The SINGING QUILT

CAN ANOTHER WOMAN'S COURAGE MOVE HER
to Try the IMPOSSIBLE?

KATHI
MACIAS

Other Fiction Titles
by Kathi Macias

"QUILT" series

The Moses Quilt
The Doctor's Christmas Quilt

"FREEDOM" series

Deliver Me from Evil
Special Delivery
The Deliverer

"EXTREME DEVOTION" books

More than Conquerors
No Greater Love
People of the Book
Red Ink

The SINGING QUILT

CAN ANOTHER WOMAN'S COURAGE MOVE HER
to Try *the* IMPOSSIBLE?

KATHI
MACIAS

NEW HOPE
PUBLISHERS
Gospel-Centered. Missions-Driven.

BIRMINGHAM, ALABAMA

New Hope® Publishers
PO Box 12065
Birmingham, AL 35202-2065
NewHopeDigital.com
New Hope Publishers is a division of WMU®.

Library of Congress Control Number: 2013955339

ISBN-10: 1-59669-392-4
ISBN-13: 978-1-59669-392-0

N144101 • 0314 • 3M1

To my beloved husband, children, and grandchildren, whose love is so precious to me, and to my wonderful Lord, who gives me a song to sing, regardless of where I am in life, or whether or not I can see the way before me.

Prologue

NOT A BREATH OF BREEZE PASSED through the steamy back alley where Jolissa Montoya sat scrunched up in the little spot she'd claimed as her own so many years earlier. For as long as she could remember, this had been her escape, her not-so-secret hideout where she ran when her world threatened to cave in and smother her—which was nearly as often now as it had been way back then.

I was a kid when I started coming here—just a kid. I should have outgrown it by now.

The self-condemning words added to Jolissa's already heavy sense of failure, as she peered out from her hideaway behind the weathered slab of wood that had once served as a gate. Now, long since torn from its original moorings, it passed as a lean-to in the dirt alley behind the ramshackle two-bedroom house in the suburb of Los Angeles Jolissa called home.

Home. What pain the word caused as it echoed through the young woman's fragile heart. The house where she'd spent the last fourteen years of her life since her parents had died when she was seven, the house where she'd been forced to grieve in silence so as not to disturb the only other occupant's self-imposed solitude, the house where her crippled uncle complained from his wheelchair that he had never wanted to raise a child, particularly such a pathetic and useless one. Could such a building truly be considered a home? Jolissa doubted it. But since she'd been orphaned at such a young age, her uncle's abode had been her only option to avoid growing up in foster care.

More than once over the years she'd wondered if foster care might indeed have been better, though she had to admit that at least her uncle had never beaten or abused her, and she'd always had something to eat, though she usually had to prepare it herself.

Her stomach growled now, reminding her that she had yet to eat anything today, and it was well past noon.

I shouldn't have slept in. Tio likes me to get up early and make him breakfast. If I had, he might have been kinder to me with his words.

Deep down, Jolissa knew that wasn't true. Her uncle was seldom in a good mood or prone to speak kind words to anyone, particularly the girl he considered the greatest burden of his life, worse even than the diving accident twenty years earlier that had severed his spinal cord and turned him into a paraplegic. "At least before you came I could suffer in privacy. Now I have to put up with you on top of having these useless legs." How often had she heard those words? Yet his voice would soften just a notch then as he added, "But you're family, after all. I had no choice."

Jolissa imagined that was true—at least so far as her uncle Joseph saw it. There were no other family members to take Jolissa in, and so her *tio* had grudgingly agreed to do so. If only he had let just one day in the last fourteen years go by without reminding her of his sacrifice! But of course, he hadn't. And Jolissa knew he never would.

She longed to stand up to her *tio* when he put her down, but she couldn't. Besides, most of the time he was right; she truly was a burden to him. But as a child, what could she have done about it? Now that she was an adult, however, shouldn't it be different?

Jolissa had always dreamed it would be. After high school she'd enrolled in the local junior college, hoping to lay the groundwork for one day becoming a social worker, helping children like herself learn to make their way in life.

What a joke! Her cheeks burned with shame at the thought. Who was she to try to help someone else when she couldn't even help herself? Each time her uncle's complaints became too great to bear and she dared to offer to move out on her own, he'd laugh and convince her that she'd never make it without him. Though a tiny corner of her heart longed to fly, to find out if maybe she really could make it on her own, the rest of her quaked in fear at the very thought.

I can't even talk to people without stuttering or slipping back into Spanish. And the way I pronounce some of my words, you'd think I'd been born in Mexico. But I wasn't! I was born right here in the United States, and I should be able to speak perfect English . . . without stuttering and making a fool of myself.

Hot tears threatened to overflow onto her cheeks, but she brushed them away. She'd just about made peace with her life as it was, with her job at Evergreen Laundry and Dry Cleaners a few blocks away—where, thankfully, she didn't have to talk to the public—and attending a handful of classes at night. Why she bothered to continue taking evening classes to prepare herself for social work, she couldn't imagine—especially during the summer months when most students took time off. But then again, what else was she to do with her time? Besides, it was September now, and nearly all the students had returned to campus.

And so she'd settled into her busy schedule of working, attending school, doing homework—and trying to cook and clean in a way that would please her uncle. For the most part, her efforts seemed to be keeping her afloat—until she met the little girl with the big, sad eyes, silently begging for her to help.

Me? Help anyone? I can't even help myself!

Jolissa had turned away from the child's plea, reminding herself that though it was likely no one better understood the girl's problems than she did, there was also no one less able to do anything about them. But the round, dark eyes still haunted her, heaping guilt upon the grief that had attached itself to her and refused to go away.

Chapter 1

"STUPID HUMIDITY! Isn't the heat bad enough? Do we have to have humidity too?" Joseph lowered his voice before uttering a curse word, but Jolissa heard it anyway. She kept her lips pressed together and went on with her dusting. Thankfully it wouldn't take long, since her *tio* wasn't one to accumulate any unneeded furniture.

"You'd think we lived in the tropics," Joseph muttered, adding another curse for emphasis.

Jolissa had never been anywhere near the tropics, but she'd seen pictures of tropical islands with white sands and blue waters, lush jungles with verdant greens shimmering in the sun, and waterfalls that took your breath away with their majesty. It was obvious their modest *casita* in the *barrio*, the little neighborhood, was nowhere close to a tropical paradise.

"You almost done there?" Joseph groused. "I'm getting hungry."

Jolissa kept her back to him and continued to work. "Al-m-m-m-m-most." Heat shot up her neck and into her cheeks as the familiar shame mocked her. "As s-s-s-s-soon as I f-f-finish these l-l-l-last couple of p-p-p-p-pieces."

"*Idiota*," he growled.

Jolissa refused to let the tears surface. After all, he'd called her a lot worse than an idiot before—and no doubt would again. But *idiota* seemed to be his favorite.

Just finish your job. Ignore him and get done. Then you can make supper. He won't die of starvation while he's waiting.

Even the vague reminder that her only living relative could die—of starvation or otherwise—brought a war of emotions to her heart. Her initial thought was that if he died, she would at last be free of his cruel words; but that momentary relief quickly morphed into crushing guilt over wishing him dead. How selfish could she be? Hadn't he taken her in when she had nowhere else to go? Hadn't he given her a place to live, food to eat, and clothes to wear? He had, and she'd heard of those sacrifices almost daily. Still, in light of that, fear gripped her heart. Where would she go if something happened to her *tio*? Could she manage on her own? Would she even know where to start? The only thing her benefactor did besides eat, sleep, watch TV, and complain was to pay the bills. The one time she'd dared to ask him if the house was paid for he'd nearly annihilated her with his words. She now knew never to ask about finances again. He had made it perfectly clear that it was his money that paid their way; the details were none of her business.

Sweat trickled into her eyes, and she brushed it away with her forearm before finishing the one bookcase in the house. It held only four books—one dictionary and three novels set in the Old West—none of which Jolissa had ever seen her *tio* pick up, let alone read.

She shook her head at the thought. Books were the best friends she had. She'd discovered at an early age how she could escape to faraway places and live as a princess in a castle or as a magical warrior, saving the world from evil invaders. The few books she'd acquired over the years were stashed safely away under her bed. She pulled them out periodically to reread them in between reading the ones she checked out at the library—and of course, her schoolbooks. But her favorite was the Bible that had originally belonged to her grandmother and then her mother. Both of them were gone now—to heaven, Jolissa hoped, assuming the Bible was right about that—but they had left behind the little black book, with its tiny printing and occasional scrawled margin note. Those notes had served to keep her connected to the book's previous owners, though Jolissa's grandmother had died when Jolisa was still a toddler, so the memories were dim.

She reached back and flipped her long, dark ponytail off her neck. Even pulling it back in a band didn't help today. The heat and humidity nearly plastered her hair to her skin.

Ignoring what she couldn't change and going back to her musings, her thoughts went from the vague memories of her grandmother to the heartbreaking images of her mother. Even now, after fourteen years, Jolissa closed her eyes and easily pictured her mother's face. Beautiful, with long, thick black hair that blew in the wind when she didn't bother to braid it or pin it up. Beautiful on the inside too—sweet and kind, friendly and full of laughter. How Jolissa missed that laughter! One of her greatest fears was that she would one day forget what it sounded like. So far that hadn't happened.

"That's enough!" The command, shot at her from the kitchen, jolted her back to the dark, cramped living room where she still stood in front of the nearly empty bookshelf. In addition to the four books, the only other contents were a half dozen old pictures of Joseph before his accident—all action photos, snapped at ball games or group outings. More surprising to Jolissa than the fact that her uncle was once young and active—something she'd never seen since he was crippled soon after she was born—was the way his face glowed in all the pictures. Whatever he happened to be doing when the camera shutter clicked, he was smiling, his dark eyes dancing with obvious delight. It was hard for Jolissa to imagine that the grumpy, bitter old man she called *Tío* had once enjoyed life.

I enjoyed it once too—before I became an orphan.

From the memory of her lovely, laughing mother, Jolissa slipped over to the vision of her strong, handsome father. She had always thought he was quite tall, though she now understood that he had just appeared that way in her little girl eyes. But at least, with him, she always felt safe. She hadn't felt that way since he died.

"Did you hear me, Jolissa?"

She flinched at the sound of her name, nearly hissed through teeth clenched in anger. Hearing herself called *idiota* was preferable to having her name spoken in such a demeaning tone.

She turned from her completed task and swallowed the lump in her throat. "I h-h-h-heard you, *T-T-T-Tío*, and I'm c-c-coming to fix s-s-s-supper *ahora*—r-r-right n-n-now."

The old man with the permanent frown lines and downturned mouth squinted at her as if trying to decide if she meant what she said.

Turning her eyes from his gaze, she carried the furniture polish can and rags past the wheelchair and into the kitchen, out onto the back porch where an old washing machine collected dirty items for her to wash later. She wished they had a dryer but knew better than to mention it. Her uncle believed there was no need for one, as they had a perfectly good clothesline out back.

Placing her cleaning items on top of the washer, she turned back to the kitchen and mentally assembled the items she would need for making leftover chicken tacos and rice. If she worked quickly, they could be eating in about a half hour. After cleaning up the dishes, she'd have to hurry to make it to school on time, but *Tío* would never allow her to leave until her work was done. If only he hadn't demanded that she dust before dinner.

She sighed. No reason to think about things she couldn't change. She would work as quickly as possible and then rush off to school. She had only one class this evening, so she'd still have time to come home and study a bit before falling into bed at last.

At least I don't have to be at work until ten tomorrow. A slight smile twitched the corners of her mouth but couldn't seem to stay in place. *At least I won't have to get up quite as early as usual to make breakfast for* Tio *before I leave.*

She turned the fire on under the skillet and dropped in a small scoop of *manteca*. It was melted and starting to sizzle by the time she'd pulled the leftovers from the refrigerator.

✳ ✳ ✳

EVA PEDROSA folded the bulletins for the Sunday service, taking care to slide an insert into each one before adding them to the growing pile. Volunteering at the Light House every Friday was one of the highlights of her week. She'd been a member of the vibrant, if modest-sized, congregation since becoming a believer nearly forty years earlier.

She smiled at the thought, as she sat alone beside the small folding table in the little cubicle off the church's main office. *Only You, Lord, could ever be so merciful to one like me. Forty-three years I went my own way, Father, but still You were faithful to pursue me and call me home to Your heart.* She sighed. *I will never stop being amazed that You, the Most High God, would love and forgive someone like me. It is indeed a miracle, Señor. A miracle!*

Eva had already made a pass through the sanctuary, making sure nothing had been left on the floor or in the pews from the midweek service. When she finished preparing the bulletins, she would leave them in the foyer for the ushers. Then she would prepare the cups for Communion as well, after checking to be sure there were enough crackers and juice for the two services.

She was nearly finished with her folding and stacking of bulletins when the nudging began in her heart—softly at first, almost a silent whisper. But as she perked up what she liked to call her "spiritual antennae," the nudging became clearer and more pronounced.

"I need to pray for someone, don't I, Lord?"

She stated her question and then waited, hoping she would find out who that someone might be. When no name or face came to her, she set the bulletins down on the table, closed her eyes, and folded her hands. "All right, Father. I don't know who it is, but You do. All I know is that You want me to pray, and that's enough."

Quieting her heart and mind so she wouldn't miss a word, she began to whisper, asking for wisdom as she prayed, protection and direction for the one she prayed for, and God's purpose and glory in it all.

✺ ✺ ✺

JOLISSA HAD MANAGED to feed *Tío* his breakfast, clean up the dishes, and get out of the house with time to spare. If only it weren't already so hot and muggy she might enjoy the five-block walk to work, but the unusual humidity continued to hang over the Los Angeles area, promising another scorcher. She'd heard a few minutes of the news this morning as her uncle watched TV while eating his *machaca y huevos*. A couple of times in the past she'd dared to mention to him that shredded beef and eggs might not be the healthiest meal each morning, but his reaction had convinced her to let him eat whatever he pleased.

She sighed now at the memory of the weather report, which indicated the heat wave wouldn't break for at least two or three more days. Longingly, she allowed her mind to wander to the thought of the ocean breeze that could usually be felt even as far inland as she was. What a relief it would be when it finally returned! She vowed never to complain about cool breezes again.

Especially when I think of what's waiting for me at the cleaners. I'm so glad to have the job, but . . .

She nearly stumbled as she briefly closed her eyes, trying to block out the anticipation of the smothering heat that awaited her in the back room where she worked. Though she normally rejoiced at not having to interact with the public because she dreaded each time she had to speak with someone she didn't know, having to endure their obvious impatience as they listened to her stutter, she would have preferred to be in the front office where the air conditioner hummed all day long.

The Evergreen Laundry and Dry Cleaners sign was just a half block ahead now, and it almost made her laugh. *Sounds like they want people to think everything is fresh and cool inside when it's anything but. "Putrid Swamp Cleaners" would be more appropriate right now.*

As she reached the front door, she steeled herself for the five-hour shift that lay ahead of her. *Today could be worse,* she told herself. *I could be working a full eight-hour day like I often do.*

She pulled the door open and stepped inside, relishing the brief blast of cool air that greeted her as she nodded a good-morning to the receptionist who was busy speaking with a customer on the phone. Jolissa stepped past the woman's desk and continued into the back room, which oozed with steam and heat and the various smells of clothes being cleaned and pressed.

After she set her purse on the break table and stuck her sandwich in the refrigerator, her boss stepped up to her, his heavyset face flushed to the hairline of his rapidly balding head.

"Jolissa," he said.

She nodded. *"B-b-buenos d-d-dias—"* Her cheeks flamed as she realized she had spoken to him in Spanish. "Good m-m-m-morning, Mr. P-P-P-Peterson." Still embarrassed, she thought of asking how he was or commenting on the weather but opted to keep her speech to a minimum. He usually seemed to appreciate that.

Mr. Peterson frowned. "I, um . . . I'm afraid I have some bad news for you."

Her heart seemed to stop as she waited. Jolissa had seldom received good news, so she steeled herself for the inevitable.

"As you've probably noticed, we . . . well, we haven't been very busy lately. I was hoping things would pick back up, but . . ."

His voice trailed off. Jolissa continued to wait, telling herself to breathe.

"I've looked at this problem every way I can," Mr. Peterson said. "I've considered letting you or Marianne go, but I really don't want to do that. But I just can't afford to pay two full-time people anymore. So I've decided to give you both the option of staying on part-time. I'll give you as many hours as I can, but it won't be forty anymore—not unless things pick up again, of course. Until then it'll probably be more like twenty or twenty-five." He paused and shrugged, his obvious discomfort increasing. "That's the best I can do. Take it or leave it."

Jolissa swallowed, the dreams of paying for continuing her education and maybe even saving a little money in the process evaporating into the oppressive moist heat that seemed to press her down.

"I'll t-t-t-take it," she said at last, knowing she probably wouldn't be able to find anything better anywhere else. At least it was something. At least he wasn't firing her entirely, which is what she'd expected from the moment he announced that he had bad news. So maybe things weren't quite as bad as she'd expected. Maybe the economy would pick back up and Mr. Peterson would give her more hours again. But what would she tell her *tio*? She still had to pay her share of the rent and groceries. That sure wasn't going to leave much for anything else . . . including school.

Mr. Peterson shoved his hands in his pocket. "I should have called you at home, but I thought it was better to tell you in person. The thing is, though, . . . I really don't need you today. Marianne is already here, and I'm going to be here all day too, so . . ." He shrugged again. "I guess what I'm saying is that you can go on home for now. I won't need you again until Monday. Can you come in then? About nine? You can work half a day, and then Marianne can work the second half."

Jolissa found herself nodding, though she felt as if she were reading his lips rather than hearing his words. Maybe it was because of the ringing that had started in her ears.

She watched him walk away and then turned back to the refrigerator, retrieved her sandwich, grabbed her purse, and headed for the exit. She didn't even notice the brief blast of cool air as she passed quickly but silently through the front office on her way outside.

Chapter 2

THE HOT, MOIST AIR SMACKED her in the face as she stepped into the glaring sunlight. Even the LA smog didn't help block the rays; if anything, it added a brown tinge to the sky and the odor of decay to the air.

Jolissa scarcely noticed it. She told herself she should go straight home. After all, where else would she go? She didn't need to be at school until six, and it wasn't even ten thirty. Still, the thought of going home to face *Tio* for the next few hours was not appealing, particularly if he started badgering her about why she'd come back so soon. She wasn't about to tell him about the cutback in her hours . . . at least not yet.

She rounded the corner and found herself less than a half block from the Light House. The modest church had always seemed to call to her when she passed by, particularly if there was a service going on. Jolissa had been drawn to the lively singing but never had the nerve to enter and try to join in, though she'd often considered sitting in the back to watch and listen.

I wonder if the door's open.

She frowned at the thought. What kind of church was open on Friday morning? The parking lot was nearly empty, and the few cars that were there could easily belong to people who were shopping or visiting nearby. Still . . .

Jolissa followed the tug on her heart and approached the few stairs that led to the main entrance. She didn't want to go into the office and risk seeing anyone, but maybe the sanctuary would be empty and she could sit there a while.

The door pulled open without resistance, and she peered inside, blinking her eyes to help them adjust to what seemed semidarkness compared to the sunlight outside. Cool, quiet, and almost dark. The temptation to enter was too strong to resist.

Before she knew it, Jolissa found herself sitting on a smooth wooden pew in the very back row. Silence surrounded her, and she felt her shoulders relax. Her eyes now adjusted to the muted light, she gazed at the front of the church. A lone wooden podium graced the middle of the otherwise empty altar area. On the wall directly behind the podium, a large cross hung on the wall. A faint odor of lemon teased her nose, and she wondered if someone had been here ahead of her, cleaning and polishing in preparation for Sunday.

She darted a glance around her, hoping that whoever had done the cleaning had finished and gone. Apparently so, as she saw no one. With a sigh she closed her eyes and allowed herself to think of the little Bible that had belonged to her mother and her grandmother. For a reason she couldn't understand, she found herself wishing she had brought it with her. She seldom read it at home, except to trace the handwriting of its previous owners. It helped her feel close to them somehow, and right now she really needed that.

"Can I help you with anything?"

The voice was so soft Jolissa thought she'd imagined it, but her eyes flew open anyway, then widened at the sight of the elderly woman standing in the aisle beside her. The woman's smile was warm, but Jolissa felt as if she'd been caught trespassing.

"*Lo s-s-siento*," she mumbled, her face heating with shame. "I'm s-s-sorry. I didn't mean t-t-t-to—"

The pleasant-looking woman, who wore bifocals and had her salt-and-pepper hair pulled back in a bun at the base of her neck, waved away Jolissa's explanation. "It's perfectly all right. The doors to the church are unlocked for just this reason—so people can come in to pray or reflect, or just to enjoy His presence." Her smile widened and she patted Jolissa's shoulder. "I shouldn't have disturbed you."

"Oh n-n-no," Jolissa protested. "It's f-f-f-fine. I sh-sh-shouldn't have—"

"Of course you should have. And I'm glad you did. Now you go right back to what you were doing, and I'll leave you in peace."

The woman removed her hand from Jolissa's shoulder and turned away.

"W-w-wait!"

Jolissa swallowed. Where had she gotten the nerve to call her back—and why?

Their eyes met again, and this time the elderly woman raised her brows. "What is it, my dear? What do you need, and how can I help?"

Jolissa hated the hot tears that sprang into her eyes, but she didn't have the energy to pull them back. Even as the first droplet spilled over onto her cheek or she could reason through her response, she whispered, "P-p-prayer? You w-w-would pray for me?" She swallowed the lump in her throat. "*P-p-por favor.* P-p-please?"

The woman's questioning expression melted into compassion as she squeezed in next to Jolissa on the pew and took her hands. "Of course I will pray for you, *mija*. I am Eva. What is your name?"

Jolissa opened her mouth twice before she could force the word out: *Jolissa*. She managed to say it without stuttering, and Eva smiled before closing her eyes.

* * *

So that's who You wanted me to pray for. Eva smiled as she stood in the church's open door and watched the young woman walk away. *Quite obviously she has no idea how lovely she is, and she certainly doesn't realize how very much You love her. Now I know how to pray for her.* She sighed. *I just hope she comes back to see me again.*

Eva was about to step back inside when she saw Jolissa stop. Hesitantly, the young woman turned and looked back toward the church. When their eyes met, a flush deepened the girl's face. Eva smiled and waved; after only a brief pause, Jolissa returned the gesture before continuing on her way.

Closing the door behind her, Eva walked down the aisle toward the front of the church. She needed to step through the side door and follow the hallway toward the little cubicle where she worked beside the main office. But the cross on the wall caught her eye, and she stopped.

"*Gracias, Señor*," she whispered, her heart swelling with the familiar gratitude of love bought at a great price. "Thank You for caring about even the sparrows that fall, about a sad young woman, so obviously filled with fear and grief . . . and about an old woman like me." She shook her head. "It's one thing that you saved me, Lord. But that You use me as well? Now that truly is a miracle."

She reflected again on how she'd been working in her cubicle earlier that morning and felt the need to pray for someone. She had done so, as much as she was able without knowing any specifics. But she had no sooner finished than she sensed a pull to check on the sanctuary. She had planned to do so shortly anyway, but the pull was urgent, so she obeyed. That's when she spotted Jolissa sitting in the back corner, her eyes closed and a look of sadness on her face that tore at Eva's heart.

"Your timing is perfect, Father. No matter how old I get or how hard of hearing, please let me have ears to hear Your voice—and a heart to obey."

Jolissa Montoya. I will pray for you, mija. *For as long as the good Lord leaves me here on this earth, I will pray for you.*

* * *

JOLISSA DREADED GOING HOME, but the stop at the church had helped. Eva Pedrosa was one of the nicest women she'd ever met. *Like the grandmother I can't remember. And I love how she prayed for me. Is it possible that God will answer? Not for my sake, but for hers—for such a good woman who spends time at the church and prays for others. Surely for her God will hear and answer!*

As quietly as possible she slipped into the house, avoiding every creaky board as she tiptoed down the hallway toward her room. She'd spotted her *tio* asleep in his chair in front of the TV and breathed a sigh of relief. If she stayed in her room, maybe he wouldn't even realize she had come home. After all, she still had her sandwich in her purse, so she could just eat lunch in her room and maybe even take a nap or get some studying done—

Or read the Bible.

Jolissa nearly stumbled at the thought, but caught herself in time to keep from banging against the wall and waking her uncle.

Read the Bible? Where had that come from? True, she'd been thinking of it while she sat in the church, but now she found herself desiring to open the pages and read more than the notes placed there by her mother and grandmother. It was obvious those two women had spent a lot of time reading the little book; maybe there was something in it that would help her too.

The memory of Eva's prayer danced through her mind as she soundlessly closed the door behind her, leaning against it in relief. The woman had prayed as Jolissa asked—that she would get more hours at work and that her uncle wouldn't find out about the situation and get angry with her. But the woman had also prayed that God would reveal Himself to Jolissa and show her how much He loved her.

How much He loves me? How is that possible? How does He even know who I am? And if He does know me, how could He love me?

The assurance that He did know sifted through her pores, warming her heart with a truth she could scarcely accept. Shaking off the unfamiliar feeling, she crossed the room toward her bed, snagging the little Bible on the way. The room was stifling, but she dare not turn on the window fan and chance waking her uncle. She would eat her sandwich and read her little book in the heat.

I'm cooler than I would be if I were at work right now. The thought brought mixed emotions, but she shoved them away. She let the book fall open and read the first line that popped out at her, printed in red ink: "Let the little children come to Me, and do not forbid them; for of such is the kingdom of God."

She gasped as the image of the little girl who had approached just a few days earlier crystallized in her mind. The child hadn't spoken, though Jolissa sensed that she wanted to. *Why didn't she? Does she stutter, like me?*

Jolissa had no answer to her own questions, but she looked again at the sentence she had read. There was a number in front of it: fourteen. What did that mean?

In the vague recesses of her memory she pulled up her mother's voice, explaining that the Bible was written in different books, then divided into chapters and verses. Perhaps that's what the fourteen meant.

She studied the page and decided the name of either the book or the person who wrote it was Mark, and that the lines she had just read were from the tenth chapter, fourteenth verse. But none of that mattered as much as the emphasis on children. Jolissa's heart ached for children, particularly those who suffered—as she had. Was it possible there were answers for these suffering children right here in the little book her mother and grandmother had left to her?

Her heart sparked at the thought, and she curled up on her bed, Bible in hand, and began to read, the oppressive heat forgotten.

Chapter 3

JOLISSA HAD MANAGED TO GET through the afternoon without her uncle realizing she'd come home early. She'd made him dinner, gone to class, and then come home and escaped once again to her room to read from the Bible until her eyes burned and she turned out the light, sleeping soundly until morning.

Now she yawned and stretched, fighting the urge to roll over and go back to sleep, but the sun was already up, and though she didn't have work or school today, she did have a lot of homework to get done.

And breakfast to make. Tio *will be up soon, if he isn't already. I'd better get his coffee made.*

She rolled to her side and sat up, sliding her feet into her raggedy but comfortable slippers. It was already too warm for a robe, but if her uncle was still sleeping, she could get into the shower before he claimed the bathroom. Because of the wheelchair, the doors in all the rooms had been widened so he could get around. Jolissa had offered many times to help him transfer to and from his wheelchair, but he refused, instead struggling on his own until the feat was accomplished, grumbling and cursing the entire time. The same held true of his morning ritual of wheeling himself into the shower, which had also been adapted to accommodate the chair, and showering and dressing himself. Jolissa always tried to get to the bathroom ahead of him, as once he was in there she knew it would be an hour or more until he came out.

Grabbing a pair of shorts and a cool blouse, she made a beeline for the bathroom, pleased to see it was empty. Her uncle's bedroom door was still closed and she could hear his snoring. She'd made it! Now to get in and out before he awoke and started pounding on the door.

She wasn't fast enough. Though she showered and dressed quickly, her *tio* was already complaining by the time she left the steamy bathroom behind and stepped into the hallway.

"It's about time," he groused, his heavy brows drawn together. "I don't ask for much in life, but I sure would like to be able to use my own bathroom when I need to. Never thought I'd have to wait for some selfish female to finish primping."

Primping? Jolissa nearly bit her tongue to keep the words from spilling out, stutter or no stutter. She hadn't had the luxury of primping since she was a little girl and played princess and dress-up with her mother. But it was useless to explain that, so she stepped past her uncle and headed for the kitchen, calling back to him as she went, "I'll m-m-make the c-c-coffee and have your b-b-breakfast r-r-ready by the t-t-time you're out, *T-T-Tio.*"

"Great! Make it now so it'll be cold by the time I get there. Brilliant! Can't you do anything right?"

She heard the bathroom door slam as she reached for the coffee pot. Fine. She'd make a cup for herself now, and then a fresh pot for him later, though he'd probably complain that she was wasting money making two pots. It seemed there was no way to please him, no matter how hard she tried. Then again, she hadn't been able to do so in fourteen years, so why did she continue to try?

Because I have nowhere else to go. I'm stuck here. Tio *is all I've got.*

A niggling thought that perhaps that wasn't true danced around the edges of her mind, but she blocked it out. She'd allowed herself to be lured by hope before, and all she'd ever gotten out of it was more pain. Best to accept the way things were and live accordingly.

She watched the coffee drip into the pot and wondered if she could stand an entire day at home, listening to her uncle complain and call her names. The image of her little hideaway in the back alley, the spot she'd made her refuge so many years earlier, danced through her mind, but she quickly dismissed it. She went there less now than she used to, but it still beckoned to her on occasion.

Not today. It's just too hot, and besides, I'm too old to sit out there in the alley and feel sorry for myself. Surely there's an alternative.

It was also too hot to take her studies to the park, but the library was only a few blocks away—a long walk on a hot day but preferable to being called an *idiota* here at home or hiding behind a broken gate in the alley. Besides, she could use a computer at the library, something she didn't have at home. Yes, after she'd fed her *tio* and cleaned up the breakfast dishes, she would head for the air-conditioned library and spend her day there.

✻ ✻ ✻

JOLISSA FELT BRUISED by the time she finally escaped the house. The midmorning sun baked her as she walked, her study materials stuffed into her worn backpack.

Why does he get so angry about me leaving when it's obvious he can't stand having me around?

She fumed as she walked, her physical burden bouncing between her shoulders with each step, even as her emotional burden chewed at her heart. Angry voices penetrated her concentration, and she stopped, glancing across the street to see two women standing on the sidewalk, arguing. But it wasn't the accusations hurled in Spanish or even the pointed gestures that drew her attention; it was the small child standing a few yards from them, her thumb in her mouth and her eyes wide, as she watched and listened.

She's heard this before. How many times? How many more times before she learns to tune it out?

The little girl with the long, stringy brown hair turned her eyes from the two women and looked directly at Jolissa, who sucked in her breath at the moment of recognition.

She remembered now. It was the same child she'd spotted a few days earlier, sitting on the stoop in front of that very house, sucking her thumb and staring at Jolissa with wide, dark eyes. The girl didn't speak then, and she didn't speak now, but Jolissa was certain she could hear her crying for help.

I want to help, mijita. *I really do! But how? It's none of my business, and besides, they wouldn't listen to me.*

She knew it was impossible from such a distance, but for a moment she imagined she saw tears glistening in the girl's eyes. Jolissa's heart squeezed with the pain of futility, as she turned away and resumed her walk, picking up her pace as she went.

There's nothing I can do, she repeated to herself, over and over again. *Nothing. Nothing!*

She'd gone several blocks by the time she stopped to catch her breath and assess her surroundings. How had she ended up here, in front of the Light House? She needed to be at the library, studying. Then again, would it hurt to take just a few moments first, to sit and reflect in the cool, quiet sanctuary?

Hoping the door would again be unlocked, she turned her feet toward the steps leading to the front door.

Eva focused on one of her favorite Fanny Crosby songs as she sat on the back pew where she'd met Jolissa the previous day.

Blessed assurance, Jesus is mine . . .

The words rang out in her heart as she hummed. At almost eighty-three, Eva often felt ancient—until she remembered that her beloved "Aunt Fanny" was still writing songs and even making public appearances and speeches right up until just a couple years before she died at the age of ninety-four. Though blind, the amazing "queen of gospel songs" wrote more than 8,000 poems, most of which were then put to music. From what Eva had read of this amazing woman, she had never once felt sorry for herself but had instead enjoyed her life and blessed thousands in the process.

She glanced down at the tattered old quilt that lay in her lap. Eva's beloved friend, Cecelia, had given it to her just days before she died. "I want to leave it with someone who will appreciate it, and I know how much you admire Fanny Crosby."

The singing quilt. That's what Cecelia had called it, in honor of the woman whose life had inspired its pattern. Cecelia had been a talented quilter and had put together more than a dozen of them over the years, gifting them to people for birthdays and Christmas. But Eva knew that the singing quilt had been Cecelia's favorite—which is why she had kept it for herself, right up until days before her death.

Eva refolded the quilt and wondered how many people had truly appreciated its significance when it was on display in the church's fellowship hall the previous month. The pastor had decided to put it up on the wall, along with pictures of Fanny and a brief biography of her life, as well as a list of her best-known hymns, to educate church members who might not otherwise know about the remarkable woman's life and contributions. At the pastor's request, Eva had just this morning taken the display down so another could take its place. She would now take the quilt home to rest at the foot of her bed.

She heard the back door open before noticing the shaft of light that briefly brightened the area where she sat. Turning her head, Eva felt her eyes widen as the young woman named Jolissa peered inside, sunglasses in hand as her own dark eyes came to rest on Eva.

Lord, what are You up to? You've had me praying for her for two days, and now here she is—again. This is too much of a coincidence to be a coincidence!

As quickly as her arthritic back and legs would allow, Eva stood to her feet, smiling as she exited the pew and headed for Jolissa. "You came back!" With the quilt tucked under her left arm, she reached out her right hand in welcome, sensing the urgency to draw the girl in before she changed her mind and left.

"I'm so glad you're here," Eva said, relieved that Jolissa had responded to her outstretched hand. Though the young woman's skin was warm, Eva sensed a slight trembling.

"I . . . I j-j-j-just w-w-wanted to come in for a m-m-minute and—"

"No need to explain, *mija*. Here, come and join me. I was just sitting here a moment myself. We may as well sit together, *sí?*"

Jolissa opened her mouth, then closed it again and nodded.

Guide us, Father, Eva prayed silently. *I don't know what needs to happen here, but You do.* Then, still clasping Jolissa's hand, she led her back to the pew where they'd sat and prayed together the day before.

Chapter 4

A MYRIAD OF EMOTIONS WARRED INSIDE Jolissa as she bounced from one to the other—primarily unreasonable fear at connecting with this woman for the second time in as many days and inexplicable relief for the very same reason. Jolissa felt drawn to this *viejita*, the old woman named Eva, even as she felt drawn to the church where they now sat. But why? Though she knew her parents and grandparents had been what she thought of as "religious," Jolissa had never seen any direct benefits from living such a life. The God they all claimed to love and serve had stolen Jolissa's parents from her when she needed them most and then sent her to live with an angry old man who despised the very sight of her. Was she supposed to be grateful for that?

And yet, since she'd begun reading through the pages of the little Bible her mother and grandmother had left her, Jolissa had to admit that she'd sensed some sort of drawing or nudging of her heart. Toward this church? Toward God? Toward the woman called Eva? She couldn't be sure, though she was admittedly fascinated with the Man called Jesus, whom she'd been reading about lately.

"Are you all right, *mija*?"

Eva's voice broke through her thoughts, and Jolissa flinched as she turned to look at her. They perched close together on the back pew, where they'd sat the day before.

Eva was turned toward her, so Jolissa responded and angled her body toward Eva until their knees were nearly touching.

"I'm f-f-fine, *gracias*. I j-j-just wanted to s-s-stop in and . . ." And what? She wasn't sure herself, so she let the thought hang.

Eva's smile was warm, crinkling the wrinkles around her eyes. "You are more than welcome here, Jolissa—always. I've been praying for you, as I promised, and I wondered how you are doing. It isn't often I run into someone here in this empty church two days in a row."

Jolissa swallowed. "I . . . I hadn't p-p-planned to c-c-come here. I was g-g-going to th-th-the library to s-s-study, but . . ." She took a deep breath and tried to think out her words before speaking them. "S-s-somehow I ended up h-h-here."

"I'm glad you did." Eva leaned a bit closer. "I believe God wants us to become acquainted, and that's much easier to do when we have a chance to spend time together."

Jolissa felt her eyebrows rise. Why would God want them to become acquainted or spend time together? Did God really care about such things?

Patches of color caught her eye, and she zeroed in on the folded quilt still tucked under Eva's arm. Had she been holding it when she took Jolissa's hand and invited her to come in and sit down? Jolissa couldn't remember.

"That's b-b-beautiful," she said, nodding with her head toward the bundle. "Did you m-m-make it?"

Eva glanced down at the quilt, then lifted it from under her arm and let it fall open on her lap. After caressing it for a brief moment, she lifted her head and smiled. "No, I didn't. But my precious friend Cecelia did. She's with Jesus now, but she gave this to me just before she left."

With Jesus? Obviously Eva's friend had died, but what an odd way to express it.

"I s-s-see. It m-m-m-must be very s-s-special to you."

"Very." Eva glanced down at the quilt and then back up again. "One of my most treasured earthly possessions. And not just because my friend made it, but also because it tells the story of an amazing woman who wrote more songs than I will ever sing if I live to be a hundred."

Jolissa sat up a bit straighter. "The quilt t-t-tells a s-s-story?"

"*Sí, mija.* A beautiful story . . . about a beautiful woman. Would you like to hear it?"

"Oh, I c-c-can't s-s-stay long. I have to g-g-g-go to the l-l-l-library to s-s-study."

Eva smiled and laid a hand on Jolissa's arm. "Then I'll just tell you a little today. If you like it, you can come back and I'll tell you more another time."

Silence hung between them, and Jolissa's heart raced. Why did she care about the story behind a quilt? Was this part of the drawing she'd felt on her heart, as if God Himself was calling her? Ridiculous! God wouldn't do that . . . would He?

And yet . . . she could spare a little time. She wasn't working or going back to school until Monday, so if she stayed a little while there would still be plenty of time to study.

"*Sí,*" she whispered, swallowing a buzz of excitement that made no sense. "I w-w-would l-l-like to hear a l-l-little bit of your s-s-story."

Eva's smile broadened and she lifted the quilt from her lap. "*Bueno.* Then we will begin at the beginning."

* * *

AS EVA BEGAN HER STORY, she watched Jolissa. It was obvious the young woman was paying close attention. Eva was pleased. She explained why her friend had called this the singing quilt, and then she positioned it so she could point out the center patch. She smiled as her admiration for the blind songwriter rose to the surface.

"This is where it all started," she explained. "And where it all ended too, I suppose, but we'll get to that later. Do you see how this patch resembles the sun?"

Jolissa nodded, and Eva continued. "Then you also see how half the sun is bright and half nearly hidden by darkness. What a perfect symbol of Fanny Crosby's birth!"

She laid the quilt back in her lap. "Fanny was born in the little village of Brewster, New York, about fifty miles north of New York City, on March 24, 1820. Her parents named her Frances Jane Crosby, but she quickly became known as Fanny. The sunshine in the patch represents the joy her parents felt the day they welcomed her into the world."

Eva paused, sensing that Jolissa wanted to say something. "Was she b-b-b-born b-b-blind?"

"Possibly. Some doctors seem to think that was the case, but the most commonly believed story is that she lost her sight when she was about six weeks old. She had a cold in her eyes and her parents were concerned, as new parents often are, particularly with their firstborn. Sadly, the family physician was out of town so they asked another doctor to examine little Fanny. They didn't know this man but trusted him. As it turns out, that was most likely a mistake. He prescribed hot mustard plasters to be put on her eyes, which apparently blinded the poor child. The man left town soon after and was never heard from again."

Tears glistened in Jolissa's dark eyes. "How s-s-sad. So she c-c-couldn't s-s-see anything at all?"

"A sliver of light now and then, that's all." Eva lifted the quilt once more. "And so my friend covered half the sun in this patch to show the darkness that came into Fanny Crosby's life while she was still a tiny baby."

"When F-F-Fanny g-g-got older and f-f-found out h-h-how she got b-b-blind, she m-m-m-must have b-b-been very angry w-w-w-with that d-d-doctor."

"Surprisingly, she wasn't. In fact, she believed God allowed it to happen to fulfill His plan for her life. And what a plan it was!" Eva smiled and patted Jolissa's hand. "He has a plan for each of our lives, you know."

Jolissa hesitated, a slight blush rising in her cheeks. Nervously she glanced at her watch. "I . . . I sh-sh-should go. I h-h-have to s-s-study." She raised her eyes to Eva. "Could I . . . come b-b-back s-s-s-sometime and h-h-hear more of the s-s-story?"

Eva smiled, her heart swelling with joy. "Of course you can, *mija*! That would be wonderful. Anytime." She pulled a small pencil and an offering envelope from the back of the pew in front of them and wrote down her number. "I don't have a cell phone, but you can call me at home so we can plan when to meet. And if you'd like to come to my home instead of meeting at the church, that's fine too. I live just a couple of blocks from here."

The young woman's eyes widened and she hesitated before reaching out to take the number. "Are you s-s-sure? I w-w-wouldn't want t-t-to impose."

Eva laid her hand on Jolissa's arm. "You would never be imposing, *mija*. I'm an old woman who lives alone except when one of my *nietos* comes to see me—which isn't often enough. I tell them their old *abuela* would like to see her grandchildren more often, but most of them are grown up now with lives of their own." She sighed. "So you see, you would be doing me a favor to come and visit me."

Jolissa's smile seemed wistful, but she nodded. "That w-w-would be w-w-wonderful. *Gracias,* señora."

"*Por favor, mija*," Eva said, leaning close, "call me *Abuela*. I am more than old enough to be your grandmother, and I would love it if you called me that."

Jolissa nodded again, rose from her seat, and then looked down shyly. "*Gracias . . . Abuela.*"

Eva watched her leave, and her heart ached as she imagined the painful story the young woman no doubt carried inside her. Maybe one day she would feel free to share it.

✸ ✸ ✸

JOLISSA SCARCELY FELT the scorching heat when she left the church and headed for the library. She was amazed to realize she could easily have sat in that pew all day, listening to Eva tell her about the blind woman named Fanny Crosby. But the part about God having a plan for each of us was more than she could process. She needed to put such a thought out of her mind and do some studying, though she sometimes wondered at the purpose of it.

Will it do any good?

The thought taunted her, as it often did. She tried to ignore it as she trudged down the block, keeping her eyes on the sidewalk and wishing she'd brought something to drink. She'd been so anxious to escape her *tio*'s foul mood this morning that an apple and a banana were all she'd snagged before leaving home. But there was a water fountain at the library; it would have to do.

Abuela. Her lips twitched into a near smile at the memory of the woman named Eva saying Jolissa could call her *Abuela.*

I don't remember my grandmother—not really. At least not enough to miss her the way I do my mom and dad. But it would be nice to have an abuela, *even if it's just pretend.*

Pretend! *Why use such a silly word at my age? I did a lot of pretending when I was little, but I should have outgrown that by now—just like hiding in the alley. I know my* tio *doesn't like me very much, but he's all I've got, and I might as well accept that and quit wishing for something better because better just isn't going to drop into my lap. I don't even know if I can study myself into it, but I have to try.*

She lifted her head then, aware of a familiar clucking sound. Sure enough, she spotted chickens in the chain-link fenced yard across the street. Apparently they were disturbed by the old woman with the broom sweeping the dirt from the small walkway that led from the gate to the front door.

Why bother? Jolissa was tempted to point out to the old woman that the chickens would spread the dirt back to the walkway within the hour, but she pressed her lips together and said nothing. Unless the woman in the dark housedress and black platform shoes was senile—and that was certainly a possibility—she already knew her task was pointless. But for whatever reason, she did it anyway.

An exercise in futility, much like my studies. But we have to try, don't we?

She turned away from watching the old woman and her chickens and continued down the street. When she arrived in front of the library, she stopped and hitched her backpack a little higher on her shoulders, and then mounted the steps.

Chapter 5

JOSEPH WASN'T SITTING in his usual spot in front of the TV when Jolissa returned home late that afternoon, though the newscast blared from the screen at its usual grating volume.

"*Tio?*" She moved past the TV, resisting the impulse to turn it off, knowing that would only annoy her uncle. "Wh-wh-where are y-y-you?"

He wasn't in the kitchen, though she saw signs of his attempts to make his own lunch. Why hadn't he just reheated what she'd left him? She shook her head, assuming he had to be in the bathroom or taking a nap.

She left her backpack in the living room and headed for the hallway. The bathroom door was wide open, though his bedroom door was closed. She listened for his snoring, but instead heard a faint moan.

"*Tio?*" Her heart leapt as she pressed her ear up against the door. She knew he'd be angry if she woke him, but her concern overrode her caution. "T-T-Tio, are y-y-you all r-r-right?"

"*Ayudame*! Help me!" The call was faint, but clear enough that Jolissa didn't hesitate another moment. If her proud uncle was asking for help, he was truly in trouble. She turned the knob and pushed open the door, immediately spotting her uncle on the floor between the side of the bed and his wheelchair.

"*Tio*, wh-wh-what h-h-happened?" She hurried to his side and knelt down. "Are y-y-you hurt? How l-l-long have you b-b-been here?"

A scowl drew his heavy brows together, and the fire that shot from his dark eyes sent a familiar stab of fear to her gut.

"Stop asking so many questions," he growled, though at a lower level than usual, "and help me get into bed. I've been here for hours, waiting for you to finally get home. What good are you anyway? I give you a roof over your head, food, clothes—everything you could want—and how do you repay me? You abandon me." He shook his head, obviously exhausted from his outburst. And yet he continued. "Don't give me that innocent look. I know better! You were off having fun while I was here suffering. You'd think after all I've done for you that you could at least take care of me in my old age. Now stop staring like an *idiota* and help me into bed."

Blinking back hot tears, Jolissa reached for his arm. "Are you s-s-sure, *Tio*? You d-d-don't think anything's b-b-broken, do you? M-m-maybe I should c-c-call an ambulance."

"*Idiota*! There is nothing wrong with me except that I can't get up. Now make yourself useful and help me."

Jolissa knew better than to argue further, so she lifted and heaved and struggled until the man who easily outweighed her by seventy pounds was finally in bed.

"Now get me something to drink," he ordered, the beads of sweat standing out on his forehead. "While you were out having a good time with your friends, I've been here on the floor, wishing for a drink of water."

Friends? The word mocked her as she turned toward the door and headed for the kitchen. The closest thing she had to a friend was Eva, who had given her permission to call her *Abuela*. She clung to the woman's gift to ease the sting of her uncle's words.

His voice called to her before she'd gotten more than a few steps away. "And after you get me something to drink, get dinner started. I'm starving!"

She let the tears flow then, as she went to the sink to get her uncle a glass of water. How she longed to be with her new *abuela* again, to hear more of the story of the blind woman told in the patches of the quilt. She clenched her teeth and nodded once to herself, remembering that Eva's phone number was tucked away safely in her backpack. Yes, she would call her tonight, after she'd fed her uncle and cleaned up the kitchen. She would ask her *abuela* when she could see her again—and then she would go, whether her *tio* liked it or not.

✳ ✳ ✳

EVA SAT IN HER FAVORITE CHAIR, close to the window where the window air conditioner worked overtime to dispel the heat. She'd come home from her visit with Jolissa just before noon, had a little lunch, and then napped through the hottest part of the afternoon. She'd heard the heat wave was about to break, and she hoped that was true. Even her cat, Mario, seemed affected by it. He usually took advantage of every opportunity to jump into her lap when she sat down, but today he'd scarcely looked at her when she lowered herself into the chair. He lay between her and the air conditioner, and it was obvious he wasn't moving any farther away from that cool air than necessary.

She smiled. "I imagine you'll get up from there when you hear me pouring your dinner into your bowl, won't you?"

Mario opened one eye and peered at her, then closed it and went back to sleep.

"Can't say that I blame you." Eva sighed. "We're just not used to all this heat and humidity, are we?"

The phone rang then, and Eva raised her eyebrows, turning to the combination phone/answering machine that sat on the table next to her chair. When her children or grandchildren came for one of their rare visits, they never failed to point out that her phone was antiquated and she should trade it in for a cell phone so she could carry it around with her.

"Why would I want to do that?" she'd asked them, but they never gave her what she considered a satisfactory answer. And so the antiquated machine continued to summon her to answer it.

She did, and smiled when she heard the familiar voice on the other end.

"*Señora?* I m-m-m-mean, *Abuela?* This is J-J-Jolissa."

"Jolissa, what a nice surprise! How are you, *mija?*"

"I'm f-f-fine, but . . . are you s-s-sure it's all r-r-right that I c-c-called?"

"Of course it is, *mija*. That's why I gave you my number. Is everything OK with you?"

Eva waited through the pause, shooting up a silent prayer before Jolissa answered.

"Y-y-yes, everything's OK. I just w-w-w-wondered if I c-c-c-could visit you again s-s-soon. T-t-tomorrow, maybe?"

Eva's heart squeezed at how painful it must have been for the girl to struggle through her questions. Had she always stuttered that way? And why hadn't someone at home or in school helped her?

She dismissed her own questions and got back to Jolissa's. "I would like that very much. But I should tell you that I go to church in the morning. Would you like to join me? We could come back here after and have some lunch."

The pause was longer this time. At last she spoke. "I . . . I d-d-don't know. I mean, I'd l-l-l-like to, b-b-but I . . . I m-m-might not be able to c-c-come early enough for ch-ch-church."

"That's just fine, *mija*. You can meet me at church at nine thirty, or you can just come here around eleven or any time after. Whatever works best for you. How's that?"

"That's f-f-f-fine . . . *Abuela*."

Eva smiled and gave Jolissa her address. "*Hasta mañana*, Jolissa. See you tomorrow, *mija*."

She hung up the phone and looked over at her cat. "Looks like we have a date, Mario. What do you think of that?"

Mario didn't answer, but Eva imagined he would somehow express his opinion when he met Jolissa the following day.

❋ ❋ ❋

ACCORDING TO THE MORNING NEWS, this would be the last day of the oppressive heat before the cool ocean breezes would once again bring more moderate temperatures to Southern California. It was the one bright spot in Jolissa's otherwise disappointing morning.

She arose early and scurried around getting her *tio*'s breakfast ready, hoping to break away in time to meet her new *abuela* at church. Unfortunately *Tio* had not cooperated. He had slept a bit later than usual, taken longer in the bathroom, and then complained that his breakfast was cold. It was one of the many times Jolissa had wished they had at least one modern convenience—in this case, a microwave, but since they didn't it had taken her several minutes to reheat the food in the oven. Then *Tio* had complained that his breakfast was dried out, and Jolissa had done her best to ignore his tirade.

When at last all her chores were done, she took a deep breath, tried to quiet her pounding heart, and announced, "I'm g-g-going to my f-f-f-friend's house. I'll b-b-b-be home th-th-this afternoon." Then she stood in front of her uncle's wheelchair, waiting, dreading the outburst that was bound to come.

Jolissa couldn't remember ever seeing her *tio* smile, but now she watched his face turn from displeased to furious. His brows drew together, and his dark eyes shot darts of displeasure that Jolissa could almost feel.

"Your *friend*?" Joseph's words came out in a snarl, and Jolissa nearly jumped. His voice rose to a roar then. "Your *friend*? And what sort of friend is this? A man, no doubt!" A string of profanity burst from his mouth then, and Jolissa felt herself shrinking in front of him. "After all I've done for you, you leave me here alone to go spend time with your *friend*? You are a terrible girl. Terrible and ungrateful! Do you think I don't know what you do with your *friends* when you are gone from here? How could you do such a thing? What did I ever do to deserve such a punishment as to have you in my house?"

Jolissa's legs nearly gave way, but she forced herself to remain standing. "I . . . I am d-d-doing n-n-n-nothing wrong, *T-T-Tio*. I will s-s-see you th-th-this afternoon."

Before he could erupt in a response, she turned and hurried for the front door, blocking out the vile words that followed her even after she'd stepped outside into the hot sunshine. Blinking back her tears, she realized she'd forgotten her purse but wasn't about to go back for it. Instead, she nearly raced for the church, wondering if she would be too late to find her *abuela*.

Will she be waiting for me? Church started nearly an hour ago. What will happen if I come in late?

The thought of walking in when the service was nearly over, imagining everyone turning to find out who had been so rude as to come in that late slowed her feet to a walk. If only she'd brought her purse. That's where she'd placed her *abuela*'s address. Could she remember it? She tried, but nothing came to her. Her only choice now was to give up and go back home, or wait outside the church until she saw Eva. The choice was a simple one.

Chapter 6

Eva had waited as long as possible on the steps outside the church, hoping Jolissa would show up. Disappointed, she'd finally gone inside alone and taken a seat in the back row, just in case the girl came after the service started. But now they sang the closing hymn, and there was no sign of Jolissa.

Maybe she'll still come to my house for lunch. Por favor, Señor, *bring her! I would truly love to spend more time with her. It is obvious, Lord, that the poor girl has a broken heart, and Your Word says You are near to those with a broken heart. Be near to her now, Father, and bring her to me, will You?*

The pastor spoke the benediction and then asked those who wanted prayer to come forward. Eva was torn. Others were streaming toward the back door, while a handful of parishioners made their way to the front for prayer. Should she join them and ask for prayer for Jolissa, or go home and wait for her there?

She stood where she was, gripping the pew in front of her and waiting for direction. At last she sensed a pull to go home, and so she stepped out into the aisle and joined the last of the stragglers heading for the door.

The sunlight blasted her eyes as she stepped outside, nearly blinding her until she placed her dark wraparound shades over her glasses. She spoke a couple of quick good-byes before glancing around on the off chance that Jolissa might be waiting for her. Sure enough, she spotted her sitting on the grass under an ancient oak across the street. When their eyes met, Jolissa stood to her feet and offered a shy wave.

Eva's heart soared. *You are so good,* Señor! Gracias a Dios!

With her Bible under one arm, she grasped the railing with her free hand and carefully descended the half dozen steps to the sidewalk. Jolissa was already there.

"*Mija*, you came!" With one arm she drew Jolissa into an embrace, sensing the young girl's trembling. She pulled back. "Are you all right?"

The girl looked stricken. "I w-w-wasn't s-s-sure I sh-sh-should come. I'm l-l-l-late and I forgot my p-p-purse with y-y-your address, so I w-w-waited and . . ."

Her voice trailed off, as tears pooled in her wide eyes. Eva reached up to caress the girl's cheek. "Shh, it's OK, *mija*. I am glad you came. We will talk of what's bothering you when we get to my house. It's only a couple of blocks from here. Come, we will go home and make lunch together. And you can meet Mario." She smiled. "He is expecting you."

She looped her arm through Jolissa's and led her down the street, speaking of the weather as they walked and praying silently all the way.

✸ ✸ ✸

"Your h-h-home is b-b-beautiful," Jolissa said as they walked through the front door and into the cool entryway.

Eva laid her hand on Jolissa's arm. "But you haven't even seen it yet."

Jolissa felt the heat climb into her cheeks. Why did she have to say such stupid things? If she wasn't careful her new *abuela* would end up agreeing with her *tio* that she was an *idiota*.

"I'm s-s-sorry," she managed to say. "I just m-m-meant it f-f-feels beautiful. P-p-p-peaceful."

Eva squeezed her arm before letting go. "Don't apologize, *mija*. I realize now what you meant, and I appreciate the compliment." She leaned closer, and Jolissa caught the faint fragrance of lilacs. "It's not the house that is peaceful, *mija*. It is the One who is honored here as Lord."

Jolissa frowned. She knew Eva was referring to God, but Jolissa hadn't heard anyone speak of Him in that way since . . . Her heart squeezed with the memory. *Since Mama and Papa died.* She blinked back tears and tried to focus on *Abuela*'s words.

"Come, *mija*, I will show you around, and then we will go into the kitchen and make something to eat. First you must meet Mario."

Mario. *Abuela* had mentioned him on the way over, but Jolissa had felt uncomfortable asking for any information not offered. Now she was to meet this man. Surely Mario was *Abuela*'s husband.

Eva led Jolissa into a small but cozy living room. A fireplace was on one wall, between two windows, one with an air conditioner blowing air that made the room quite comfortable. An adjacent wall boasted a large picture window looking out onto the street. Below the window was a dark blue sofa, its arms and back covered with lace doilies. Across from the couch and picture window sat a navy brocade recliner, also sporting lace doilies. A dark mahogany end table, which closely matched the coffee table and held an old-fashioned phone with a built-in answering machine, was next to the recliner. The entire room seemed to be built around the colorful braided rug at its center.

But . . . where was Mario?

"Meow."

Jolissa heard the plaintive cry at the same moment she

felt something soft brush up against her pant leg. Startled, she peered down at a small, sleek gray cat, purring as it rubbed against her.

"*Aye, mija*, Mario has already welcomed you!" The old woman beamed and shook her head. "He never takes to people so quickly. This is very unusual."

Inexplicably, Jolissa felt her heart swell, and she bent down to pet the cat. "*Buenos dias*, Mario. *Como estas?*" Out of habit, she quickly corrected herself and switched back to English. "H-h-how are you?"

She glanced up at Eva. "M-m-may I p-p-pick him up?"

Eva's eyebrows were arched and her eyes wide, as she nodded. "*Si, mija*. Of course. But . . . did you notice you hardly stuttered when you spoke to Mario?"

Jolissa blinked. Was it true? No, she hadn't noticed. But how was that possible?

Her face grew heated again. "I . . . I d-d-didn't n-n-notice." She swallowed, unsure what to say next.

Eva laid a hand on her arm. "I'm sorry, *mija*. I shouldn't have said anything."

Jolissa shook her head. "It's O-O-OK. I j-j-just didn't r-r-realize."

Eva nodded and smiled. "Go ahead and pick up Mario. I think he would like that very much."

Jolissa hesitated, then bent down and lifted the soft bundle into her arms. She stood up and faced Eva as she stroked Mario's fur, marveling at his loud purr. "I l-l-love animals."

"And they love you, I can see." Eva turned. "Come. You can bring Mario while I show you the rest of the house."

After a short tour of the two bedrooms and one bathroom, the two women and one feline made their way into the kitchen. Jolissa's initial sense of peace had been confirmed, as she took in the humble but warm decor. The house was very nearly the same size as her *tio*'s, but so much more attractive and welcoming.

"*Por favor, mija*, sit down." Eva indicated the small table in the corner, surrounded by four chairs. "I made enchiladas last night. All I have to do is put them in the microwave, and we'll be eating in no time."

Once again Jolissa lamented the fact that they had no microwave at home, but this time, as she cuddled Mario and watched Eva take the tray of food from the refrigerator, it didn't bother her so much. She found herself thinking this was one of the very best days she could remember in a very long time—maybe the best since before her parents died.

"What would you like to drink, *mija*?"

The enchiladas were now in the microwave, and Eva stood by the open refrigerator, waiting for an answer.

"Anything is f-f-fine," Jolissa answered. "Please d-d-d-don't go to any t-t-trouble."

Eva laughed. "Oh, *mija*, it's no trouble to pour two glasses of water or tea. It is a blessing for me to have you in my home."

They settled on ice water, and Jolissa's mouth began to water as the aroma of Eva's wonderful cooking filled the air. Thoughts of *Tio* and all she faced at home soon faded from her mind as they shared their lunch, with Mario perched on her lap the entire time. Jolissa soon knew of Eva's late husband, Guillermo, and their five grown children and seemingly countless grandchildren, none of whom visited Eva as often as she would like. Jolissa told Eva of her job at the cleaners, including that she'd recently had her hours cut. She also mentioned, though she tried to keep it casual, that she was taking some classes at night, in hopes of going into social work one of these days. But she carefully avoided any mention of her uncle, except to say she had lived with him since her parents died in a car accident.

"Oh, *mija*, I am so sorry to hear that!" Once again *Abuela* laid her hand on Jolissa's arm. "How old were you when it happened?"

Jolissa gulped, hoping she could answer without breaking into tears. "S-s-s-seven." Before Eva could take the thread of conversation farther, Jolissa asked, "H-h-how old is M-M-Mario?"

She watched the woman's expression as she processed Jolissa's quick change of subject. After a moment she smiled and answered. "He's very old for a cat—nearly thirteen. My *esposo* got him for me when he was just a tiny kitten. I was pleased but surprised. Guillermo wasn't much for pets, so we never had any, other than a few fish in a tank for the children. Then, two weeks after Guillermo brought Mario home, he had a heart attack and died." She glanced down at the cat in Jolissa's lap. "I think of Mario as a gift from God and Guillermo to help me through the terrible loss I felt when I became a widow."

Her eyes flickered then and her smile faded. "I am so sorry, *mija*. Losing a husband in my old age can't have been nearly as hard as losing both your parents."

How had they gotten back on that subject? Jolissa was nearly frantic to change it. "The qu-qu-quilt. I've been th-th-thinking about it. Could you t-t-tell me m-m-m-more of the s-s-story?"

Eva's eyebrows lifted. Jolissa knew she had surprised her with another abrupt change of topic, but talking about her parents was something Jolissa simply was not able to do. But the story behind the quilt? That was safe. She could handle that.

"I would be happy to tell you more about the story behind the singing quilt." Eva smiled and stood up. "Have you had enough, *mija*? Do you want more?"

"Oh, no, *Abuela*, I'm very full, *gracias*." Gently she lifted Mario from her lap and set him on the floor, where he meowed once and then padded over to a bowl of dry cat food and one half full of water. "I'll help you clean up while Mario has his lunch."

Eva laughed. "There isn't much to do, but *sí*, let's do it together and be done quicker. Then you and I and Mario can go into the other room, and I will tell you about the next patch on the quilt."

✻ ✻ ✻

MARIO HAD ONCE AGAIN CURLED UP ON JOLISSA'S LAP, purring as he dozed. Eva sat at the opposite end of the blue sofa, the singing quilt between them. Jolissa had to remind herself not to hold her breath as she waited for her *abuela* to begin. Eva's smile warmed Jolissa's heart, and she watched closely as the old woman lifted the quilt in her gnarled hands.

"Do you remember this patch in the middle, the one of the half-darkened sun?"

Jolissa nodded. "Y-y-yes. It s-s-symbolizes F-F-F-Fanny's birth and th-th-then her b-b-blindness."

"Exactly." Eva moved her finger to point to a patch with a tree on it. "Do you see this tree?"

Jolissa nodded again, wondering what part a tree could possibly play in a blind woman's life.

"This represents Fanny Crosby's family tree—her parents and her ancestors before that." She laid the quilt on the sofa and fixed her brown eyes on Jolissa, rearranging her glasses before continuing. Her long black-and-gray hair was braided and twisted around the top of her head, instead of in a bun at the nape of her neck as it had been the last couple of times Jolissa had seen her. The old woman's eyes squinted in her wrinkled face, as if she were about to stress something very important. Jolissa leaned forward, not wanting to miss a word, though she still wondered why this story had become so important to her.

"You see, *mija*, blindness wasn't the only difficulty to come into Fanny's life while she was still a baby. She was not quite a year old when her father, John, died, so the poor girl grew up without even a memory of him." Eva sighed, as a look of sadness passed over her face. "Maybe that's why she was so deeply devoted to her heavenly Father. Whatever the reason, she never spoke much about her father or his side of the family. Many thought it was because she was embarrassed about the fact that her parents were thought to have been first cousins."

Jolissa raised her eyebrows. Cousins? *Primos?* The thought that if her *tio* had ever had children they would have been her cousins darted through her mind, but she quickly shoved it away.

"Because of her father's death when Fanny was so little, she was raised exclusively by her mother, Mercy, and her side of the family, including her maternal grandmother." She smiled and patted Jolissa's hand. "Her *abuela*. The three of them were very close. And despite the fact that Fanny avoided the mention of her father or the family ties between her parents, she was still quite proud of her Puritan heritage."

"P-P-Puritan h-h-h-heritage?" Jolissa knew about the Puritans, of course, but she wasn't sure what Eva meant about Fanny Crosby's heritage.

Her *abuela* nodded. "She was very patriotic and loved to announce that her ancestors were Puritans, claiming that her family tree was rooted in and around Plymouth Rock. One of her ancestors, Simon Crosby, came to this country in 1635 and was one of the founders of Harvard College."

Jolissa had certainly heard of Harvard, though she couldn't imagine ever going there, let alone being descended from one of its founders.

"Because some of Simon's descendants married into the *Mayflower*'s families, Fanny became a member of the Daughters of the Mayflower and also of the Daughters of the American Revolution. She considered both memberships a great honor."

Jolissa tried to picture herself being part of an exclusive group because of her ancestors, but she couldn't come up with any likely scenarios.

"She had other well-known ancestors as well. Fanny eventually became an ardent abolitionist, so she was quite proud to have been descended from Presbyterian minister Howard Crosby and his abolitionist son, Ernest Howard Crosby." Eva's smile broadened. "And of course, her later relatives would also include the famous singers Bing Crosby and his brother, Bob."

Jolissa felt her cheeks warm. Famous? She'd never heard of them before but was too embarrassed to say so.

Eva chuckled. "Don't worry, *mija*. Only a *vieja* like me would remember Bing Crosby. You're far too young!" She rolled her eyes. "But, oh, how dreamy he was and how he could make us swoon 'back in the day,' as they say now."

She wanted to tell her *abuela* that she was not a *vieja*, an old woman, but of course she was. Instead, Jolissa smiled and nodded. "I w-w-would have l-l-liked to hear M-M-Mr. Crosby sing."

Eva's face lit up and her eyes danced. "And you certainly will! I'm nearly done with the part of the story that applies to the tree, so I will finish it and then get out my old records. I can't wait to show you how handsome Bing Crosby was, and what a smooth voice he had." She leaned forward. "All the young girls were crazy about him."

Jolissa giggled, nearly startling herself as she realized how seldom she laughed out loud. "I w-w-would l-l-like that."

"Well, then," Eva continued, "let's go on with the story of Fanny's family tree. Let's see, where were we?"

She paused, and then nodded as she continued. "Eunice Paddock Crosby was Fanny's grandmother, and the one who introduced Fanny to the Scriptures and helped her develop a strong faith in God at an early age. She helped Fanny memorize large sections of the Bible and quickly realized what a bright mind the girl had. Sadly, she worried that her granddaughter would never get much of an education because of her blindness." She shook her head. "That was one of Fanny's greatest concerns as well. She often said that it caused her more sadness than anything else in her life—even her blindness and the loss of her father." Eva paused. "The blind received little or no education in those days, which truly was a tragedy."

Jolissa nodded. With all the grief and torment she had endured in her own life, she knew how much she appreciated being able to read and study, whether anything ever came of it or not.

"Well, now," Eva said, sitting up straight, "I think that about covers that part of Fanny's story. Would you like to hear one of Bing Crosby's albums now?"

"Y-y-yes." Jolissa nodded, still stroking the purring feline in her lap. "I w-w-w-would l-l-like that very m-m-much."

Eva smiled and pushed herself up from the couch. "Wait right there. I'll be back in a minute."

Chapter 7

THOUGH THE MUSIC SEEMED ANCIENT, Jolissa had to admit that the crooner's voice soothed her. She could see how he might have made young ladies swoon "back in the day," as her new *abuela* said. The three of them—Jolissa, Eva, and Mario—had sat on the sofa, listening to the music for more than an hour. The scratchy 78 RPM records had been put away now, and Jolissa began to worry that she had overstayed her welcome.

"I . . . I sh-sh-should be going. I need t-t-to . . ."

Her voice trailed off. What did she need to do? Go home to her *tio* and listen to him shout at her again, to tell her what an ungrateful *idiota* she was? However, the memory of him falling and lying on the floor, waiting for her to come home, stabbed her with guilt. Maybe she really did need to go after all.

"*Mija*, can you stay just a little longer?" Eva smiled. "I have some *flan* in the refrigerator. It would be a perfect dessert, don't you think?"

Jolissa's mouth watered. She'd hadn't had *flan* since her mother died, but the faded memory was enough to make her salivate with anticipation.

"My m-m-mother used to m-m-make *flan*. I l-l-l-loved it, b-b-but I d-d-don't know how to m-m-m-make it."

"Then we shall eat some now, and some other time when you come over I will teach you how to make it yourself."

Jolissa felt her eyes widen. "You w-w-w-would d-d-do that for m-m-me?"

"I would be happy to, *mija*." She leaned close. "You would be giving me a great blessing. My daughters and grand-children aren't interested in learning such things. It would be wonderful to teach you." She grunted a bit as she pushed herself up from the sofa. "Come. We will sit in the kitchen and have some now."

Mario awoke as Eva stood up. Raising his head and yawning, he hopped down from Jolissa's lap and followed Eva into the kitchen. Jolissa did the same.

"Here, *mija*," *Abuela* said, pointing toward the second shelf in the cupboard beside the refrigerator. "Get two of those little glass dessert bowls, will you? I'll get the *flan*."

Jolissa marveled at how easily and comfortably the two of them interacted in the kitchen. Would she and her mother have done similar things if . . .? Jolissa swallowed the lump in her throat. *If I hadn't become an orphan. But I did, and now all I have is* Tio. She reached for the dessert bowls. *And* Abuela. *Now I have her too. How is that possible? I didn't even know her until a few days ago.* A pang of fear shot through her heart at the thought that this kind old woman could slip out of her life as quickly as she'd slipped in. Jolissa shook her head. No, she could not allow herself to think of that now.

She set the bowls on the table. Within moments Eva had brought spoons and the baking dish full of *flan*. Like the enchiladas, Jolissa noticed that the woman wasn't serving her leftovers. It was obvious she had prepared the food specifi-cally to share with her. But why would she do such a thing?

The first taste of the creamy dessert dispelled all doubts and questions from her mind. "This is d-d-delicious! Oh, *Abuela*, w-w-will you r-r-really t-t-teach me how to m-m-make this?"

Eva laughed. "*Mija*, of course I will! And the enchiladas too, if you wish. We will have many days together, learning about one another, hearing the story of Fanny Crosby, sharing meals." She laid down her spoon and reached over to place her hand on Jolissa's arm. "*Mija*, God has brought us together for a purpose. Remember I told you He has a plan for each of us?" She smiled. "This is part of it. From before the beginning of time, our wonderful Father has planned for us to meet and to become friends—no, more than friends. Family. I don't know what will come from it, but I know it will be good because His plans for us are always good."

Tears sprang to Jolissa's eyes, and she wondered why. Was it simply because a complete stranger had been so kind to her, even to the point of "adopting" her as a grandchild—or was there more? Thought she didn't understand it, she sensed it had to do with the plans Eva mentioned—good plans, especially for her. But how could that be? Jolissa believed in God, certainly. Her parents had taken her to church as a child and had talked to her about God's love for her, but that all seemed so far away now—in another lifetime. Now she had only *Tio*—

She glanced at her watch and gasped. "Oh, *Abuela*, I r-r-really m-m-must go. It's l-l-late and I have to f-f-fix d-d-dinner for my t-t-tio."

"Of course, *mija*. I understand. Maybe next time you can tell me about your *tio*. I would like to meet him one day." She pushed back her chair and stood up. "For now I will fix you a plate to take to him—some enchiladas and *flan* for dessert. I'm sure he will like them, *sí*?"

Jolissa couldn't think of anything that her uncle really liked, but one thing she knew for certain. They were not going to talk about him the next time they got together, and she certainly wasn't going to allow her brand-new *abuela* to meet her *tio*. It would ruin everything.

"WHERE HAVE YOU BEEN?" The roaring question hit her full-fury as she walked through the front door, stunned to see *Tío* sitting in his wheelchair in the entryway, rather than in his usual spot in front of the TV.

Jolissa opened her mouth but couldn't force out any sounds. Her uncle's face was contorted with rage, and the veins on his neck looked ready to pop. Still, she couldn't find the strength to answer him.

He squinted his eyes. "You've been out with your friends again, haven't you? And not just girls. Don't deny it! I know you've been sneaking around, doing shameful things." His voice lowered only slightly. "*¿Por qué?* Why would you behave this way? Haven't I provided for you all these years? I didn't have to, you know. I didn't even have to let you come and live here. But I am a good man, an honorable man. I did what was right for my sister and took you in. And look how you repay me."

Jolissa's mind whirled. She knew his accusations were illogical, but she trembled so that she knew she would never be able to answer him in a way that would make him listen. Even when he wasn't angry and she wasn't terrified, he seldom listened to anything she said. Today would only be worse.

Skirting his wheelchair she hurried to the kitchen, intent on fixing a quick dinner. Maybe he was just hungry. Maybe if she gave him some dinner he would settle down.

It was then she remembered what was in the bag she carried—leftover enchiladas and *flan*. She was sure her *tio* would love them, though he'd never admit it.

She heard the slight squeak of one of the wheels as her uncle rolled his way toward her, but she ignored him as she turned on the oven and pulled the food from the bag, setting it on the counter.

"Where do you think you're going?" His voice was close now, and she didn't have to turn around to know he was right behind her. "How dare you ignore me? Who do you think you are, disrespecting me this way?"

Her hands still trembling, she picked up the disposable aluminum tray full of enchiladas, ready to place them in the oven. As she turned from the counter to step to the oven, her uncle reached up and knocked the tray from her hands. Stunned, Jolissa watched, as if in slow motion, while the tray flew from her hands to the floor, sauce and pieces of enchilada flying, before everything landed with a splat. The tray was facedown, having splashed sauce in all directions. It was obvious the food was ruined.

Tears pricked her eyes as she turned to the man in the chair, whose dark eyes glared at her, ignoring the mess on the floor. "Wh-wh-what have y-y-y-you d-d-d-done? M-m-my *abuela* s-s-sent that t-t-t-to y-y-you."

"Ha!" He nearly spat the word at her, as his expression morphed to mockery. "You have no *abuela*. You have only me!" And with that he stretched to the bowl of flan on the counter and swept it to the floor, right beside the ruined enchiladas.

It was more than she could take. Leaving her furious uncle and the food mess behind, she raced from the kitchen to her room. But there was no lock on her door, and she couldn't bear the thought of being trapped there if he came in and began to scream at her once again. Spotting the little Bible on the stand beside her bed, she snatched it up and sped out the front door, avoiding the back door off the kitchen where her *tio* still sat, no doubt stunned that she had left him there.

"Come back here!" His shout echoed at her as she retreated to her spot in the back alley. She might be too old to resort to such hiding places, but right now it was the only refuge she had. And at least she knew he wouldn't follow her there.

✳ ✳ ✳

THERE WERE STILL A FEW HOURS OF SUNLIGHT LEFT, yet the heat didn't seem quite as oppressive as it had the last few days. Jolissa ignored the rivulets of sweat that trickled from her thick hair and onto her face, as well as under her armpits and down her back. Her only regret was that she was sitting in the dirt in one of the few decent pairs of slacks she owned. It would have been nice to change first, but there had been no time. She'd needed to escape, and she had—for a little while, at least. She refused to think of what she would face when she finally got up the nerve to go back in the house. No doubt the mess in the kitchen would be waiting for her, but it was the fact that her uncle would still be waiting for her that bothered her most.

She shook her head. *I can't think of that now. I can't! Help me, God!*

The realization that she had just asked God for help came as a surprise, and she glanced down at the little black Bible she held in her lap. She caressed the soft leather and wondered how many times her grandmother and mother had done the same. They had loved this book, and she somehow sensed she could come to love it as well if she spent more time reading it.

Abuela *was carrying a Bible when she came out of church this morning. I wonder if she reads it often.*

She flipped the book open to the middle and found the word *Psalms* written at the top of the pages. *How do you say that word? I wonder what it means. Maybe I can ask* Abuela *next time I see her.*

The thought that she would be able to see the old woman again soon encouraged her heart, and she scanned the pages. Psalm 91 caught her eye, and she began to read.

He who dwells in the secret place of the Most High
Shall abide under the shadow of the Almighty.
I will say of the LORD, "He is my refuge and my fortress;
My God, in Him I will trust."

She nearly gasped at the thought that the words seemed to have been written by someone who was hiding from danger— not in a back alley but by trusting God. How did that work? How could God, who was so big and powerful and so very far away, help someone as small as a human being, trapped here on earth? She read on.

Surely He shall deliver you from the snare of the fowler
And from the perilous pestilence.
He shall cover you with His feathers,
And under His wings you shall take refuge;
His truth shall be your shield and buckler.
You shall not be afraid of the terror by night,
Nor of the arrow that flies by day,
Nor of the pestilence that walks in darkness,
Nor of the destruction that lays waste at noonday.

Feathers? Wings? Jolissa could almost picture herself hiding under the wings of a large bird, though she felt somewhat disrespectful imagining God in such a way.

A thousand may fall at your side,
And ten thousand at your right hand;
But it shall not come near you.
Only with your eyes shall you look,
And see the reward of the wicked.

She gasped. The reward of the wicked? What did that mean? Would her *tio* one day answer to God for his treatment of her? The thought shot a shiver up her spine, even in the heat.

Did she dare to imagine that these words from this ancient book could somehow be applied to her life?

> Because you have made the LORD, who *is* my refuge,
> Even the Most High, your dwelling place,
> No evil shall befall you,
> Nor shall any plague come near your dwelling;
> For He shall give His angels charge over you,
> To keep you in all your ways.
> In their hands they shall bear you up,
> Lest you dash your foot against a stone.
> You shall tread upon the lion and the cobra,
> The young lion and the serpent you shall
> trample underfoot.

Angels. Jolissa had heard of angels many times, but she thought they were something like fairies or elves—certainly not real. Had she been wrong? Was it possible such beings truly existed and that they might somehow protect her?

> Because he has set his love upon Me,
> therefore I will deliver him;
> I will set him on high, because he has known My name.
> He shall call upon Me, and I will answer him;
> I will be with him in trouble;
> I will deliver him and honor him.
> With long life I will satisfy him,
> And show him My salvation.

Because he has set his love upon Me. The phrase seemed like a condition, as if all the promises of protection hinged on whether or not you loved God.

Did she? She wasn't sure. She believed in his existence, of course, and in many ways she feared Him. But love Him? How could she when she didn't even know Him?

The sound of bicycles and children's voices interrupted her thoughts, and she held her breath as they passed by. She'd been discovered in her hideout several times throughout the years, usually by children who had ventured into the alley as a shortcut. More than once they'd mocked her, but she'd learned to ignore them. This time they didn't seem to notice her, as their voices trailed off and she released the air she'd held in her lungs.

Turning back to the Bible that still lay open in her lap, she read and reread the words, "Because he has set his love upon Me." *How do I do that, God? I think I would like to do that, but I don't know how.*

With that she closed the book, leaned her head against the rough fence that served as the back of her crude hideaway, and wondered how it was possible to know God well enough to love Him.

Chapter 8

JOLISSA HAD FINALLY DRAGGED HERSELF back into the house soon after sunset. The mess was waiting for her on the floor, and her uncle had maneuvered himself back into the living room and parked in front of the TV. She had braced herself for the onslaught, but none came. Joseph didn't speak a word to her the entire evening, despite the fact that she'd fixed him a sandwich and set in on a tray next to his chair. He still hadn't spoken to her when she retired to her room, and she had at last fallen into an exhausted sleep.

The alarm clock jangling in her ear dragged her back to reality, and she was relieved to realize she was going to work today. And there were classes in the evening, though that left a window of time in between. She dreaded the thought of coming back here to endure either her uncle's vicious tirades or his cruel silence. But she would deal with that later. For now she would shower and dress and leave breakfast for her uncle before heading to the cleaners.

The house was silent that morning as she went about her preparations. She was used to the TV blaring while she made breakfast, but *Tío* hadn't come out of his room even when she was ready to leave for the day.

Should I check on him? The memory of him lying beside the bed a few days earlier nudged her to walk down the hall to his room. She pressed her ear up against the door and heard his snores. Relieved, she headed toward the front door, snagging her lunch and backpack along the way.

Good-bye, Tio. A stab of guilt at not waiting around until he woke up nearly pushed her back inside, but a glance at her watch convinced her that there was no time. She'd already had her hours cut at work; she couldn't risk losing the job altogether.

She was halfway down the block when she realized she wasn't sweating. A slight breeze tossed her long, dark hair, and though the sun was warm, it didn't feel as if it were burning her skin. Best of all, the humidity was gone.

Jolissa breathed a sigh of relief. Though she would have to go home and face her uncle sooner or later, at least the morning was starting off with a hint of promise.

✳ ✳ ✳

AFTER FOUR HOURS in the back room at the cleaners, during which she made up for not sweating during her walk to work, Jolissa was off. She glanced at her watch as she stepped out into the sunshine. One o'clock. That left a lot of time before her first class this evening. Should she go home? Probably. Making lunch for *Tio* might help soothe him a bit.

Not much, though. If only he hadn't thrown the food on the floor, I could have left the enchiladas for him to heat in the oven.

She sighed as she headed away from work. She'd fixed him another sandwich and left it covered in the refrigerator before she left, so there was no sense in going home yet. It wasn't like her *tio* was going to starve in her absence.

Jolissa lifted her eyes and realized she was only a couple of blocks from the park. She could always go there and eat the sandwich she'd made for herself and stuffed into her backpack that morning. Or . . .

The thought of her *abuela* and Mario and the peaceful little home where they lived drifted into her mind. Did she dare go back so soon, especially without calling first?

I'm probably one of the few people in the world who doesn't have a cell phone. If I did, I could call. But since I don't . . .

She got to the corner and hesitated. If she continued straight ahead she would come to the park in a matter of minutes. Or she could turn left and take a chance that *Abuela* would be home and would welcome her, despite the fact that she hadn't called ahead.

It's always best to call first, she told herself, settling in for a personal argument. *It's the polite and thoughtful thing to do. But . . . I don't have a phone with me. That means I take a chance and go now, without calling, or wait and call her from home and maybe go see her tomorrow.*

She pictured herself having lunch at the park and then going home to deal with her *tio* until it was time to go to school . . . or visiting with *Abuela* and Mario.

Squaring her shoulders and taking a deep breath, she turned left and headed down the sidewalk.

✱ ✱ ✱

"*Mija*, you have come back!" The welcome on Eva's face erased all doubt in Jolissa's heart. She had indeed made the right decision.

Ushered into the entryway, the old woman insisted Jolissa come into the kitchen for a cold drink. "It's cooler today, but still warm to be out walking in the sun. Sit down while I get some lemonade from the refrigerator."

The icy liquid soothed Jolissa's parched throat, and she wondered how someone could be as kind and loving as her new *abuela*. Had she always been that way? Jolissa wished she had the nerve to ask.

"So what have you been doing today, *mija*? What has brought you here to visit with me?"

Jolissa's cheeks warmed. "I'm s-s-sorry. I sh-sh-sh-should have c-c-called first b-b-but I d-d-don't have a cell ph-ph-phone and I was c-c-c-coming from w-w-work and—"

Eva laid her hand on Jolissa's arm. "You don't need to apologize or explain yourself." She smiled. "I am very glad you're here." She glanced down at the sound of an approaching *meow*. "It looks like Mario is glad too."

Jolissa set her glass down and picked up the cat, pleased that he immediately began purring and settling into her lap as she stroked his short, silky fur.

"He's a b-b-b-beautiful c-cat."

Eva chuckled. "I think so too, but most wouldn't agree. I love his plain gray color and his intelligent look, as if he knows what you're thinking, but he's certainly not a purebred." She smiled and sighed. "But then, neither am I." She chuckled again.

Jolissa smiled in return, but wondered what qualifications were required to make an animal—or a person, for that matter—a purebred. Whatever they were, she was sure she didn't have them. Maybe that's why she thought Mario was so beautiful.

"So, *mija*, you never finished telling me what you've been doing today. Did you go to work? It seemed like you mentioned something about that yesterday."

Jolissa nodded. "Just for a f-f-few hours this m-m-morning. I used to work f-f-full t-t-time, but n-n-now our hours h-h-have been c-c-cut because b-b-business is s-s-slow. So I left at l-l-l-lunchtime and was g-g-going to eat m-m-m-my sandwich at the p-p-park, b-b-but—"

Eva's dark eyes widened. "Oh, *mija*, I am so sorry! You haven't had lunch yet, have you? I should have offered you something as soon as you got here." She pushed her chair back and stood up. "I still have some of those enchiladas in the refrigerator. It will only take a minute to heat them in the microwave."

"Oh, n-n-n-no," Jolissa protested, embarrassed that her *abuela* might think she'd been hinting that she wanted something to eat. "I h-h-have my s-s-sandwich with m-m-me. I d-d-didn't mean for you t-t-t-to fix s-s-something."

Eva was already pulling the tray of enchiladas from the refrigerator. "Don't be silly, *mija*. I know you weren't hinting, but why eat a sandwich when you can have enchiladas?" She turned, her eyes sparkling. "And I still have some *flan* too. When we finish what's in here, you can help me make a new batch so you can learn how."

Jolissa watched as *Abuela* grabbed a plate from the cupboard and began to scoop enchiladas from the pan. In less than a minute the plate was turning in circles in the microwave.

"So," Eva said, smiling as she returned to the table, "tell me about your uncle. Did he enjoy my cooking?"

Heat rose to Jolissa's cheeks. How could she explain what had happened? She'd never told anyone about her uncle, the way he treated her, how much he despised her, how afraid she was of him, though he'd never laid a hand on her. What would this kind woman think if she knew?

Tears bit her eyes, and she bowed her head, trying to blink them back. It was no use. They spilled from her eyes and onto her cheeks, then dripped down onto the table. Jolissa's shoulders heaved, but she couldn't stop herself. When *Abuela* scooted her chair closer and drew her into her arms, Mario didn't even move.

"Aye, *mija*," Eva crooned. "It's OK. Let the tears come. Let the pain out. I will listen if you want to talk. If you don't, I will just sit with you while you cry."

Jolissa had no idea if she'd be able to say anything to *Abuela*, even if she wanted to, but knowing the old woman with the kind heart would sit with her while she cried seemed one of the best gifts she'd ever received.

Chapter 9

AN HOUR LATER, when Eva had gathered together snippets of Jolissa's story between her sobs and stutters, the old woman's heart ached. It was bad enough for a young child to lose a parent, but both of them? And then to be sent to live with a foul-tempered man who obviously had no affection for his own niece? Eva imagined that Jolissa had held back on telling her how truly abusive her uncle's behavior and words were toward her, but she had said enough to let Eva know that the young woman's life was extremely difficult.

Oh Father, show me how to love her and help her—what to say and not say. Wisdom, Señor, por favor!

She handed Jolissa another tissue as the girl wiped her face yet again. The tears seemed to be slowing down now, and her sobs had nearly subsided. Eva uttered words of support and encouragement as she listened, but had otherwise kept her words to a minimum. Now she waited, not wanting to run ahead of the Lord in her desire to help.

Mario had long since abandoned the emotional exchange, and the two women sat nearly in one another's laps, their chairs drawn together until their knees touched. Eva's back ached as she leaned forward, holding Jolissa's hands in her own.

"I . . ." Jolissa began to talk, and then paused, frowning before starting again. "I'm s-s-sorry to be such a b-b-baby.

My *t-t-tio* says I should g-g-grow up and act m-m-m-my age."
She shook her head. "I'm t-t-trying, b-b-but—"

Eva interrupted by reaching up to stroke Jolissa's cheek.
"Shh, *mija*. There is no need to apologize. We never get too
old to cry. And we all need someone who will love us and
listen to us when we do. I am very glad that God has allowed
me to be that person for you."

Slowly, Jolissa nodded, the hint of a sad smile twitching
one corner of her mouth. "S-s-so am I."

Eva felt the girl tremble as she took a deep breath.
Before either of them could speak again, Mario sauntered
into the room, glanced at his empty food dish, and meowed.

"I should feed him," Eva said, watching Jolissa's
reaction. "And you too. Those enchiladas have gotten cold
again by now, but I have more. Are you ready?"

Jolissa's smile broadened slightly. "I . . . I think s-s-so.
Can I f-f-feed Mario while you get th-th-the enchiladas?"

Eva's heart swelled. "Yes. Absolutely! Here, let me show
you where it is."

Gratefully she leaned back, easing the pain in her back.
She stood slowly and turned to the cupboard where she kept
Mario's food. Hearing Jolissa rise from her own chair, Eva
smiled. *Thank You,* Señor. *Our* mija *has a long way to go, but
I think she has taken a big step today.*

"*Abuela?*"

Eva turned. "Yes, *mija?*"

"Do you think you could tell me another story about
Fanny Crosby while Mario and I have our lunch?"

Tears of joy pricked Eva's eyes. "*Sí, mija*. I would
be happy to tell you more about the wonderful queen of
gospel songs."

✳ ✳ ✳

JOLISSA THOUGHT THE WARMED-OVER ENCHILADAS were every bit as good as they were when *Abuela* first made them, and she nearly winced at the thought of how her *tio* had thrown them on the floor. But she refused to think of him now. Instead she would listen and learn more about this blind woman who had accomplished so much.

"This beautiful flower patch," Eva said, holding up the quilt, "represents Fanny's early childhood. Though she couldn't see nature, she dearly loved it. She played outside as much as any sighted child, learning to love the fragrances and feel of different flowers and trees. She enjoyed other children, and even played games with them, such as 'hide-and-seek.' Fanny never thought of herself as handicapped. In fact, she considered herself quite blessed."

Abuela reached out and patted Jolissa's arm. "No doubt that had a lot to do with the strong faith of both her mother and grandmother. Her mother worked to help support the family, so her grandmother took over much of Fanny's care and training. They spent a lot of time studying the Scriptures together, and at her grandmother's urging, Fanny memorized huge sections of the Bible."

Jolissa laid her fork down. "D-d-do you th-th-think she knew P-P-Palm 91?"

Eva frowned until a light seemed to come on in her eyes. She smiled. "Ah, you mean Psalm 91. The *P* is silent. Yes, she certainly knew that very popular psalm. But how do you know it, *mija*? Did you hear it somewhere?"

Jolissa hesitated, only slightly embarrassed at her mispronunciation of *psalm*. She swallowed. "I have a B-B-Bible at home. It u-u-used to be m-m-my mother's and g-g-grandmother's. I n-n-never read it b-b-before, b-b-b-but now I'm t-t-trying to r-r-read it a-a-and understand it."

Eva's smile seemed to spread across her entire face. "*Mija*, that's wonderful! Oh, I'm so glad to hear this! You must bring it next time and we can read it together. We will start with Psalm 91 and any other passages you've read and had trouble with." She patted Jolissa's arm again. "What a precious gift your mother and grandmother have left you. Why, just look how much you have in common with dear Fanny Crosby, who also had a godly mother and grandmother."

Jolissa couldn't imagine that she had anything in common with someone who had overcome and accomplished so much in her lifetime that she would be known as the queen of gospel songs, but she had to admit that there was a definite connection with the influence of mothers and grandmothers. *Except that mine are dead.* The thought nearly started the waterworks again, but she willed the tears away and nodded, hoping Eva would continue with the story.

After a brief pause, Eva returned to her story and Jolissa returned to her meal as she listened.

"When Fanny was three, they moved to North Salem, New York, where her grandmother had grown up. Then, a couple years later, her mother took her to see Dr. Valentine Mott, who was considered the best eye specialist in the country. It cost more money than the little family had, but friends and neighbors contributed to the journey, all hoping that the doctor could help her." Eva's face fell. "Unfortunately, there was nothing he could do. He said the condition was permanent. Fanny's mother was devastated, but the news didn't seem to phase Fanny at all. She was such a cheerful, positive child that she just accepted it as what God had purposed for her and went on with her life."

Jolissa forgot her food for the moment, stunned that a five-year-old child could remain cheerful in the face of such a challenge. Had she been too young to understand how difficult her life would be? Maybe that was the reason she didn't become discouraged or depressed.

Maybe it had something to do with Psalm 91.

The thought popped in and out of Jolissa's mind so quickly she wondered if it had originated with her—or somewhere else. She would have to read the psalm again when she got home.

"What h-h-happened th-th-then?"

Eva smiled. "The child continued to play with her friends and learn the Scriptures at her grandmother's knee, never once complaining about her inability to see. In fact, when she was eight she wrote her first poem. Would you like to hear it?"

Jolissa raised her eyebrows in surprise and nodded. That an eight-year-old could write a poem was another point of amazement in this ongoing story of Fanny Crosby, and Jolissa couldn't wait to hear it. "Y-y-yes, p-p-please."

Eva smiled. "I'll be right back. I have it in my room."

While she was gone, Jolissa peeked over at Mario, who had curled up on a small braided rug in front of the stove. He looked so contented. All he needed was to be fed regularly, petted occasionally, and then he drifted off into a sound sleep. How she longed to have such a simple peace!

Abuela returned, carrying a book. "This is one of several books that tell of Fanny Crosby's life. I'll read the poem to you." She opened the book, found the page, and darted a quick glance and smile at Jolissa before she began. "It's brief, but full of sunshine and promise." She looked back down at the book. "'O what a happy soul am I! Although I cannot see, I am resolved that in this world, contented I will be. How many blessings I enjoy, that other people don't. To weep and sigh because I'm blind, I cannot and I won't!'"

After a moment the old woman lifted her head, and Jolissa could see the hint of tears in her eyes. Her voice was hushed when she spoke. "What a thankful attitude she had. It makes me ashamed that I would ever complain. God has blessed me with so much." She shook her head and smiled.

"Once, when she was asked as an adult if she resented not being able to see, she said she did not because she knew that when she finally opened her eyes in heaven, the first face she would see would be her beloved Savior's."

For a brief moment Jolissa found herself wrestling with the thought that she too might be blessed, and yet it was too foreign a concept for her to grasp. Since her parents had died, she considered herself one of the most unlucky and pathetic human beings on the earth. *Blessed? Jolissa Montoya?* A ridiculous thought.

"D-d-didn't she f-f-feel b-b-bad about anything?"

Eva smiled. "As a matter of fact, she did. She easily accepted her blindness and the fact that her father had died before she was old enough to remember him. But there was one thing that caused her much concern and grief."

Jolissa raised her eyebrows again. "What w-w-was it, *Abuela*?"

"It was her concern that she would never receive an education like other children. Fanny had a longing to learn, an insatiable appetite for education, but there were few schools that taught the blind in those days. The best she could hope for was what her mother and grandmother could teach her at home. And yes, that one thing made her very sad."

Jolissa understood about being sad. "S-s-so wh-wh-what did she d-d-d-do?"

Eva's eyes lit up. "God provided a way for her—as He always does. But that will take us to the next patch. Do you have time to hear it today? You mentioned earlier that you had classes tonight."

Jolissa felt her eyes widen, and she glanced down at her watch. It was nearly four o'clock! She'd had no idea it was so late. She must hurry if she was going to have time to get home and make supper for *Tío* before going to school.

"I'd b-b-better not. I w-w-want to, but I h-h-have to get g-g-going. Can we s-s-save it for n-n-n-next time?"

"Of course we can, *mija*. Any time you wish. And if you can't call first, that's all right. You can almost always find me here or at the church." She smiled. "You're welcome in either place."

Somehow Jolissa knew that was true, but a familiar sense of fear was beginning to rise up inside her as she thought about going home before her class.

"May I pray for you before you leave?" Eva asked, setting the book down and reaching her hands toward Jolissa.

Once again Jolissa blinked back tears. She nodded and took her *abuela*'s hands, welcoming the peace that came as they made the connection.

✳ ✳ ✳

JOLISSA FELT HER SHOULDERS RELAX as she stepped inside the house and heard her uncle's snores echoing down the hallway from his room. Perfect! Maybe she could get dinner done and on the table before he woke up.

She scooted into the kitchen and pulled a pork chop from the fridge. *Only one left. I'll have to remember to go to the store tomorrow.* She grabbed a frying pan and turned on the gas beneath it. While it heated up, she grabbed a can of vegetables from the cupboard. Would *Tio* want tortillas with this? More than likely. She retrieved a couple of those too, and then tossed the meat in the now sizzling pan and shook a bit of seasoning on it. It would be a quick, easy dinner and, if she put some salsa on the table, her *tio* would dump it on whatever she gave him anyway.

In less than twenty minutes the meal was complete. She had just enough time to wake her uncle and then head off to class.

She turned, startled to see Joseph, parked in his wheel-chair, just a few feet away from her. How had she not heard him come in?

"*T-T-Tio*." She swallowed. "I th-th-thought you were s-s-s-still s-s-sleeping."

He sneered. "I'm sure you did. You thought you'd put my food on the table and then sneak back out to go see your friends."

"Oh no, *T-T-Tio*." Her head felt light, and her heart raced. "I w-w-w-was g-g-going to w-w-wake you b-b-before I left for s-s-school."

Joseph's eyes narrowed. "School, huh? That's what you say when you want to go out at night." He wheeled himself to his spot at the table. "I'm ready. Bring my food. And don't forget the salsa."

Jolissa exhaled. Maybe she would get off easily after all. She'd give him his dinner and then leave. Maybe he'd be asleep by the time she got home. Her heartbeat began to return to normal.

She set his plate and the salsa before him. "Wh-wh-what would you l-l-like to d-d-drink?"

"A soda," he answered without looking up, already cutting a piece of meat. "Three ice cubes. And don't give me any of that diet stuff."

Quickly she obeyed, then turned to go to her room and retrieve what she needed for her class. "I'm l-l-leaving now, *T-T-Tio*. I n-n-n-need to get to s-s-school."

"Wait."

She froze in place and turned back to him. He still didn't raise his head.

"You say you're going to school?"

"Y-y-yes, *Tio*."

She heard him smirk, but said nothing.

"So, if you are going to school, you have a teacher."

Jolissa frowned. What was he trying to say? She took a deep breath. "Y-y-yes."

His gaze still fixed on his plate as he wrapped a bite of meat in a chunk of tortilla and spooned salsa on top of it. "Good. Then bring me a note from that teacher—tonight. I want him to tell me that you are truly in school, in his class."

Her frown deepened. "B-b-but, *Tío*, wh-wh-why do you w-w-want a n-n-note? You have s-s-seen my r-r-registration papers."

He stuffed the tortilla-wrapped chop in his mouth and spoke around it. "Of course I have seen them. Who do you think pays for your so-called school? But that doesn't mean you're still going there. If you leave this house tonight, I want a signed note from your teacher when you get home. And don't think I won't call the school tomorrow to make sure he really is your teacher and not your boyfriend writing the note."

Squelching the temptation to remind him that she too contributed to the cost of her education and ignoring the almost ridiculous implication that she had a boyfriend, she said, "M-m-my t-t-teacher is a w-w-woman."

Tio slammed his fist on the table, and his plate jumped. Jolissa nearly did as well. This time he turned to glare at her. "I don't care who the teacher is. Just bring me a signed note that you are in class tonight, and I will call the college tomorrow and make sure you're not lying to me."

Jolissa's cheeks flamed, and hot tears bit her eyes. Why would he think she lied to him? Why did he doubt she was going to school? And why did he hate her so?

"I w-w-will bring you the n-n-note." Before the tears could escape onto her cheeks, she turned and rushed to her room, grabbed her things, and ran out the door without a backward glance.

Chapter 10

JOLISSA STRUGGLED TO CONCENTRATE on the lecture, but her mind wouldn't cooperate. All she could think of was the shame she would feel when she went to her professor after class and asked for a note, verifying that she had indeed been in attendance. How could her uncle require such a thing of her? She was no longer a child. Didn't he understand that?

Of course he didn't. And he never would—not so long as she continued to live under his roof. But what else was she to do? It would have been difficult enough to move out and pay her own way when she was working full time at the laundry, where she made just above minimum wage. But now that she'd been cut to part time? It would be impossible. And even if she found a second job, she'd have to quit school. Then what? What sort of future could she ever hope to achieve?

She closed her eyes and hung her head. Who was she kidding? Her heart might long to work with children, but her mouth would never cooperate. Jolissa Montoya would never be successful at anything when she couldn't speak even a single sentence without stuttering.

Rustling papers and shuffling feet alerted her to the fact that class had been dismissed. A low level of chatter buzzed through the room as students exited the class. In moments she was the only one left in her seat—except for Dr. Conglin, who sat behind her desk, jotting notes as she leafed through papers.

Summoning every bit of strength and courage possible, she pulled herself to her feet, picked up her belongings, and lifted one leaden foot after another until she reached the front of the room. When Mrs. Conglin didn't look up, Jolissa cleared her throat.

"Um, M-M-Mrs. Conglin?"

Jolissa's heartbeat echoed in her ears as she waited. At last the middle-aged woman with short, graying brown hair raised her head. A dim hint of recognition passed through her pale blue eyes. Frowning, Mrs. Conglin removed her reading glasses. "Yes? What is it? How can I help you?"

Jolissa realized the woman didn't remember her name, but she brushed that aside, determined to get her question out and the situation over with as quickly as possible.

"I . . ." She swallowed. "I n-n-need a n-n-note."

The woman's penciled-on brows rose. "A note? What sort of note?"

Once again Jolissa's cheeks were on fire, and her mouth felt dry. "M-m-my *t-t-tio—*" She shook her head and tried again. "M-m-my uncle w-w-wants a n-n-note s-s-saying I was h-h-h-here tonight."

The woman's eyebrows nearly shot up off the top of her head. She opened her mouth, paused, and then shut it again. She gave a quick nod. "Fine. Remind me of your name."

"J-J-Jolissa M-M-M-Montoya."

Mrs. Conglin grabbed a blank sheet of paper from her desk, scribbled a few words, signed it, and then folded it and handed it to Jolissa. Her brows were drawn together now, and her lips pursed. Jolissa sensed that she wanted to say something to her, but she was glad she didn't.

Taking the paper, she shoved it into her backpack, hoisted it over her shoulder, and exited the room, feeling Mrs. Conglin's stare burning a hole in her back.

Tuesday actually started out with a bit of a chill in the air, as a thick layer of gray fog hung over the LA basin. Jolissa scarcely noticed as she and *Tío* made their way through the morning in silence. She laid out his breakfast on the table, right next to the note from Mrs. Conglin. *Tío* had been in his room when she got home the night before, so she had placed it on the dining room table where it still sat in the morning. If he'd read it, he hadn't commented on it. She prayed he wouldn't follow through with his phone call to the college to confirm the teacher's identity and Jolissa's presence in the class. That level of humiliation was nearly impossible to imagine. But for now she was relieved to escape the house unscathed, with no new verbal assaults replaying in her mind.

Halfway to work she realized she should have grabbed a sweater, but she wasn't about to go back for one. She'd warm up once she hit the back room at the cleaners; for now she'd just walk a bit faster.

The day passed without incident, and by the time she emerged in the early afternoon the sun had burned through the fog. A slight offshore breeze made her walk quite pleasant, and once again she contemplated eating lunch at the park or going to *Abuela*'s. Since she had a test that evening she opted for the park where she could study while eating her sandwich.

She had almost arrived at her destination when she sensed someone watching her. Slowing her pace, she directed her gaze across the street. The little girl with the big, sad eyes sat on the stoop in front of a run-down house, her head in her hands and her elbows resting on her knees as she stared at Jolissa.

Searing pain pierced Jolissa's heart. *Oh,* mijita, *I am so sorry I haven't answered your cry for help. But what can I do? I don't even know what the problem is.*

The frail child's gaze held Jolissa in place as she fought with the desire to cross the street and talk to the girl. For a moment the child looked hopeful, but then fear won out and Jolissa turned away, ashamed as she continued to the park. By the time she reached the bench under the huge old oak tree with the widespread limbs, the sunshine seemed to have lost its warmth.

Jolissa plunked down on the bench and pulled a book from her backpack, determined to put the girl out of her mind and study for her test. For more than an hour she labored to do so, but haunting eyes and silent cries interrupted her until, at last, she turned without thinking to God.

Help her, God. Please! Forgive me for not taking a chance and talking to her. I just don't know what to do. But You can help, God . . . can't You? I know You can. Please do it, God! Please help that little girl.

A sense of peace flowed over her even as she wondered how she'd had the courage to approach such a big God when she'd been too frightened to do the same with a tiny girl.

Abuela. I must talk to her and tell her about this. She'll understand, and she'll know what to do.

With that she stuffed her book in the backpack and left the park behind.

✴ ✴ ✴

EVA WAS PLEASED BUT NOT SURPRISED when she opened her front door and found Jolissa standing there, backpack in tow. With a heartfelt embrace, she ushered the young woman into her home. Within moments they were settled at the kitchen table, with Mario happily purring on Jolissa's lap.

"Are you sure you don't want something to eat, *mija*?"

Jolissa shook her head. "I b-b-brought a s-s-sandwich and ate it at the p-p-p-park b-b-before I came. I j-j-just w-w-wanted to ask you s-s-something."

Eva waited. When Jolissa didn't continue, she laid her hand on her arm. "What is it, *mija*? You can ask me anything you wish. You're safe here."

Tears pooled in Jolissa's eyes, and she nodded. Willing herself to open her mouth, she did her best to describe the little girl she'd seen several times now, a child whose silent pleas for help seemed to follow her, even to bed at night.

"I w-w-want to h-h-help her, b-b-but I d-d-don't know what t-t-to do."

Abuela nodded, her heart aching over Jolissa's confusion. "I understand, *mija*. It is very hard to know what to do in a situation like that. But God has allowed you to become aware of this little girl for a reason. Maybe someday He will give you the opportunity to talk with her and help her in some way. But for now . . . " Eva paused and took a deep breath. "Maybe . . . maybe God just wants you to pray for her."

Jolissa's eyes widened, and Eva sensed a shiver pass over the young woman. "I . . . I d-d-did. I p-p-prayed for her while I w-w-was at the p-p-park. B-b-but I d-d-don't know if I p-p-prayed right."

Eva's heart swelled. *Oh God, You are so good!*

Before she could respond, Jolissa continued, hanging her head as she spoke. "I asked God to f-f-forgive me for n-n-not h-h-h-helping. I t-t-told Him I d-d-didn't know h-h-how to help, b-b-but I knew He d-d-did. I asked Him t-t-to h-h-help her."

Tears stung Eva's eyes, and she squeezed Jolissa's arm. "That was perfect, *mija*. Just the right prayer. And God will answer—just as He will answer the other prayers in your heart."

Jolissa raised her head. Eva could tell from the girl's expression that she was puzzled. "God hears our silent cries for help, much like you sensed from the little girl you saw, except that our Lord knows the words and feelings and thoughts behind those silent cries. And He knows exactly how to heal our pain."

Jolissa's eyes widened again, and Eva sensed she had hit a nerve. An invisible hand restrained her from going further. *Not yet.* The words whispered in her heart, and she knew she'd said as much as she was supposed to for now. Yet she knew there would be another time soon.

"So, *mija*," Eva said, forcing an extra note of cheer into her voice, "are you ready for another story about Fanny Crosby? I can go get the quilt and tell you about the next patch."

A slow smile spread across Jolissa's face. *"Sí, por favor, Abuela.* I would like that very much."

Eva nodded and rose from her seat to retrieve the singing quilt.

Chapter 11

JOLISSA WAS QUICKLY COMING TO LOVE the colorful patches of the now familiar quilt, and she found herself leaning forward in her chair—as much as she could with Mario still perched in her lap. She studied the patch showing what appeared to be a small, old building of some sort, as she waited for her *abuela* to explain.

"This represents the next portion of Fanny's life, some of her happiest years." She pointed to the patch. "Do you recognize what type of building this is?"

Jolissa shook her head, her cheeks warming as she wondered if it was something she should know.

Eva smiled. "Most people your age wouldn't. It's an old-fashioned one-room schoolhouse, though hardly the type of school that Fanny ended up attending." She laid the quilt back in her lap. "As I told you, the one regret Fanny had was her inability to go to school with the other children. She desperately wanted to learn, but there were so few opportunities for a blind child in those days."

She sighed and settled back in her chair before continuing. "When Fanny was about nine, she and her mother and grandmother moved to Ridgefield, Connecticut. Again, with Fanny's mother out working during the day, it was her grandmother who spent the most time with the child, helping her to memorize Scripture and challenging her to learn as much about other topics as she possibly could. Some say Fanny knew the entire Pentateuch—the first five books of the Old Testament—and the Book of Ruth, plus many of the psalms and most if not all of the Book of Proverbs, the Song of Solomon, and quite a bit of the New Testament by heart, and could recite it all without missing a beat. Isn't that amazing? Still, Fanny's education was limited—until just before she turned fifteen."

Mario stirred, and without taking her eyes off Eva, Jolissa stroked the cat's soft fur, which caused his motor to rev up until he drifted back off. What could have happened to change Fanny's situation? She waited, anxious for Eva to continue.

"It was the most wonderful gift anyone could have given to a girl so eager to learn. Her mother came home one day and announced that she had enrolled Fanny in a state-financed school called the Institute for the Blind. It was in New York City, and Fanny would have to leave behind her home and all that was familiar to her in order to go there. The thought may have intimidated Fanny slightly, but not enough to hold her back from accepting such a wonderful opportunity. Her first reaction was to thank God for answering her prayer about getting an education."

New York City? The idea of going to such a place on her own made Jolissa's insides churn. *And I'm an adult—plus I can see! How could she have been so brave?* She yearned to ask but didn't want to interrupt the story, so she sat quietly, her hand still resting on Mario's fur.

Eva smiled then, and Jolissa sensed the woman knew what she was thinking. It made her cheeks heat up with embarrassment to think her *abuela* could tell what a coward she was.

"As it turned out, Fanny ended up staying at the school for more than two decades, first as a student and later as a teacher." She leaned forward a bit. "So you see, *mija*, God answered her prayers in a remarkable way—just as He will answer yours if you will just begin to ask Him."

Jolissa wanted to believe her *abuela* was right. She knew the woman wouldn't lie to her, but why would God answer the prayers of someone like Jolissa Montoya in the same way He answered them for a talented, faith-filled woman like Fanny Crosby? Fanny was blind and Jolissa had trouble speaking, and they each had faith-filled mothers and grandmothers, but beyond that Jolissa could think of nothing they might have in common. Still, she was enjoying learning about this brave woman, and she hoped *Abuela* would continue to tell her the entire story.

"Don't think it was all easy for the young girl," Eva cautioned. "At first Fanny struggled terribly with homesickness. She missed her mother and her grandmother so much, and on top of that she had to learn her way around in a new environment. Of course, the other students were blind too, and it didn't take her long to make friends and to begin to feel at home at the school. Best of all, being there opened many opportunities for her."

Jolissa raised her eyebrows. "Wh-wh-what kind of opport-t-tunities?"

"Fanny had always longed to write poetry. Her teachers didn't especially encourage her dream to write, but others did." Her voice became almost hushed as she said, "In fact, it was P. T. Barnum who published her first poem. Sometime after that, the great American poet William Cullen Bryant himself visited the school, and after he had the chance to read some of Fanny's poems, he was very positive about her writing and encouraged her to continue. She later said that Mr. Bryant had no idea how much he had helped her to persevere."

P. T. Barnum? William Cullen Bryant? This blind girl had dealings with such people? How was that possible? Again, the promises from Psalm 91 teased her memory, but she dismissed them, seeing no obvious connection.

"From that point on, there was no stopping her. Fanny wrote poems and verses nearly every day. Before she knew it, she was being published in the *New York Herald,* the *Saturday Evening Post,* the *Clinton Signal,* the *Fireman's Journal,* and the *Saturday Emporium.* In 1844, when she was twenty-four and still at the school, she published her first book, *The Blind Girl, and Other Poems.* She used some of the money she earned for her writing to help fund the school that she had grown to love so much over the years."

"She wrote a b-b-book when she was t-t-twenty-four? I'm t-t-twenty-one and I c-c-c-could n-n-never write a b-b-book."

Eva took Jolissa's hand in hers. "*Mija,* we have not all been called or gifted to do the same thing. Fanny wrote poetry. God has something else equally wonderful for you to do."

Jolissa swallowed the lump that had popped into her throat. "Do y-y-you really th-th-think so, *Abuela?*"

Eva squeezed her hand. "I know so. God loves you. He has always loved you, and He will always love you. He had plans for you before the world began, and they are good plans. The Bible promises us that."

God loves me. He has plans for me . . . good plans. Oh, how Jolissa wanted to believe it! But how could she? Her parents were dead, her *tio* hated her, and she couldn't even talk to people without stuttering. How could anything good ever come from her life?

Yet she had to admit that hearing about all that Fanny Crosby had accomplished while she was blind made Jolissa dare to hope that maybe, just maybe, at least one good thing might happen for her one day too.

"Now don't think there weren't hard times for Fanny during those years, and she wasn't always the perfect little angel either." Eva grinned and leaned closer, her eyes twinkling. "You know, she might not have been able to see, but she found ways to get into mischief all the same. She loved playing pranks on people—nothing mean or destructive, of course, but little practical jokes that she quickly became famous for. But for the most part she was a top-notch student who loved to learn and who never hesitated to walk through every open door God presented to her—and she had some wonderful experiences because of it. Next time I will tell you more about some of those adventures. Would you like that, *mija*?"

"V-v-v-very m-m-much, *Abuela*. But n-n-now I have t-t-to go h-h-home."

Eva's smile faded slightly. "I understand, *mija*. But first we will pray together, *sí*? We will make that our habit. I will pray; but if you ever want to pray yourself, please do. All right?"

Hesitantly Jolissa nodded, though she doubted she would ever have the nerve to pray out loud. Still, she appreciated her *abuela* saying she could.

* * *

Tio DIDN'T SPEAK TO HER when she came home that afternoon. He sat in front of the TV while she prepared his supper and then ate in silence, as did she. It was uncomfortable, but preferable to his angry outbursts. She realized he might never tell her whether or not he'd called the school as he'd threatened to do, and she wasn't about to ask him.

She made it through class that evening without incident and then hurried home and escaped to her room to study before going to sleep. She propped her pillows against the wall and opened her notebook.

Psalm 91.

There it was again. Why did it seem to call to her?

She picked up her Bible from the stand beside her bed and flipped to the page she'd folded over and read the first line: "He who dwells in the secret place of the Most High."

The secret place? What does that mean? The secret place. It's a key to understanding the rest of it, I'm sure. I've got to remember to ask Abuela *about that when I see her again.*

A pang of disappointment stabbed her heart. Her *abuela* had invited her to come to church with her the next evening, but Jolissa couldn't miss class . . . could she? She frowned. She'd never missed yet, no matter how hard a time her *tio* had given her about going, and she was caught up on her studies. She wouldn't be missing a test if she skipped the class and went to church. But . . . was it what she really wanted? Would she feel out of place there? What if people talked to her? She stuttered worse in strange places around people she didn't know. What would they think of her?

She set the Bible aside and retrieved her notebook. Time to study. She would deal with the church issue tomorrow.

※ ※ ※

WEDNESDAY MORNING HAD COME AND GONE, and still Jolissa hadn't come to a decision about whether or not to skip class and go to church with her *abuela*. But just in case she did, she decided not to stop at Eva's for a visit after work that day and to go straight home instead. She would stick around in case *Tio* needed anything, do a little studying, fix dinner, and then head out the door, deciding then whether she would head for school or church.

"Jolissa, where are you?"

The booming demand startled her, as she sat on her bed, reading one of her textbooks. She'd left the door to her room open so she could hear her uncle if he called her, but the way he'd hollered at her she imagined she could have heard him if she were outside hiding in her little spot in the alley.

Apprehensive, she laid her book aside and dragged herself from the bed. *What could he want? It's only four o'clock, way too soon for dinner.*

As she entered the living room and spotted him sitting in his wheelchair, staring at the television, she realized this was the first time he'd spoken to her since the evening he'd demanded she bring a note from school and threatened to call to confirm her attendance. She took a deep breath and walked up beside the wheelchair.

"Y-y-yes, *Tio?*"

He didn't move, yet she was certain he knew she was there. She waited. After a couple of moments she tried again. "*T-T-Tio?* Did you c-c-call me? Do you n-n-n-need s-s-something?"

This time he lifted his head and fixed a disgusted stare on her, causing her cheeks to burn with shame. How was it her *tio* could make her feel so small with just a word or an expression?

"Of course I called you, *idiota*. Who else lives here?" He shook his head. "And why else would I call you if I didn't need something?"

She waited again. Would he tell her what that something was, or would he force her to guess?

"Are y-y-you hungry? D-d-do you w-w-want something t-t-t-to eat?"

He squinted his eyes, and Jolissa thought she could feel daggers coming from them, straight to her heart.

"I am not hungry. Not yet anyway. But I will be soon. Why haven't you started dinner? I suppose you were too busy hiding in your room and talking to your friends to care if I got anything to eat tonight or not."

She refrained from pointing out that the only phone in the entire house was the one in the kitchen, attached to the wall and certainly not portable, which made it impossible for her to talk to her friends while she was in her room. She knew from experience that defending herself in such a manner only worsened his mood.

"I w-w-was p-p-planning to f-f-fix you some l-l-leftover chicken, *Tio*. It w-w-won't take l-l-long."

He gestured as if he were spitting on the floor to his right. "Leftovers. With all the money I give you for groceries, you can't fix me something better than that? Ungrateful *idiota*!"

He turned his face back toward the TV, and Jolissa knew the conversation was over. Despite the early hour she went to the kitchen to start dinner. She decided to fix a salad and some rice to go with the chicken. Maybe that would improve his mood a bit.

Even with the extra preparation time, dinner was finished and on the table before five. "Your d-d-d-dinner is r-r-ready, *T-T-Tio*," she called from the kitchen.

In less than a minute he had wheeled himself into the room and sat glaring at the plate full of food that waited for him on the table. "It's not even five o'clock. You know I never eat this soon."

Jolissa felt her eyes widen, momentarily forgetting the futility of arguing with her uncle. "B-b-but y-y-you called me and asked m-m-m-me about d-d-dinner."

"I asked you about it, yes." He leaned forward in his chair, and though Jolissa knew he couldn't stand up and come after her, she stepped back nonetheless. "That doesn't mean I wanted you to fix it right away. I just wanted to make sure you weren't going to run off like you always do at night and forget to feed me. Do you have any idea how hard it is for me to fix my own meals when I'm stuck in this chair?"

"I . . ." Jolissa swallowed. Of course she knew how hard it was for him to do things for himself. She'd been doing all the cooking in the house almost from the time she'd come to live with him. "I'm s-s-sorry, Tio. I sh-sh-should have r-r-r-realized."

Joseph gave a quick nod. "Yes, you should have. Now get me some salsa and then leave me alone. I don't want to look at your face while I eat . . . which I will do even though I'm not hungry yet."

Jolissa retrieved the salsa and placed it on the table, then gratefully escaped to her room. She started to sit down on the bed but then changed her mind. She had done all she could for *Tio*, and she had no desire to stick around any longer than she had to. She scooped up her study materials, stuffed them into her backpack, and exited the house before *Tio* could stop her.

Chapter 12

SHE WAS STANDING on her *abuela*'s front porch before she realized she hadn't really dressed the way she probably should for church. Maybe she should turn around and leave before . . . too late. The door was open and *Abuela* was smiling at her. "Come in, *mija*! Come in! I am so glad you decided to come over. Does this mean you have decided to go to church with me tonight?"

Jolissa's cheeks flamed. "I r-r-really hadn't decided yet wh-wh-when I left h-h-home." She glanced down at her faded jeans and short-sleeved top. "I sh-sh-should have changed c-c-clothes f-f-first. Maybe I should j-j-just go b-b-back and ch-change."

Eva took Jolissa's arm and ushered into the house. "You are just fine the way you are. Our church is very informal, especially on Wednesdays. No one will be dressed up, so you'll fit right in."

Jolissa glanced at her *abuela*'s beige slacks and flowered blouse. Eva caught her glance and laughed. "Don't judge by what I'm wearing, *mija*. I'm too old to run around in jeans, but you're not. You'll be just fine, I promise. Now come, let's have a cold drink and visit a little before we go, shall we?"

They stepped into the kitchen, where Eva plopped ice cubes in two glasses and then filled them with cold water. "Do you want to sit in here? It's so nice today I thought we could go outside and enjoy the nice weather. What do you think?"

Jolissa nodded. "Outside would be fine." She took the glass from Eva's outstretched hand. "Thank you."

The old woman had scarcely opened the kitchen door that led outside when Mario appeared behind them, meowing his welcome.

Jolissa turned and leaned down to pick him up with her free hand. "I don't suppose he can come outside with us, can he?"

"Of course he can. Mario is well trained. He could climb the fence, but he doesn't. Come, let's all go out together."

A slight breeze welcomed them as they settled into the padded redwood chairs in the small patio area. A matching picnic table sat in the corner, with a bench on each side. Jolissa wondered if *Abuela* ate out here often.

"What a perfect day!" Eva sighed and took a sip of her drink, then set the glass on a small round table between their chairs. Jolissa followed her lead, setting the glass down so she could pay attention to Mario, who had already taken up residence on her lap. A faint, sweet smell of roses in full bloom helped Jolissa relax as she stroked the feline's silky coat.

"How was work today, *mija*?"

Jolissa lifted her head and found *Abuela* smiling at her. She shrugged. "F-f-fine. I w-w-wish I could get m-m-more hours, b-b-but I'm glad I s-s-s-still have a j-j-job."

Eva nodded. "Yes. There are many people out of work these days. Do you like your job?"

Jolissa paused before answering. Like her job? She liked having a job but had never really thought about "liking" what she did. "I g-g-g-guess so. I m-m-mean, it's a t-t-t-tough job, s-s-standing on my f-f-f-feet all d-d-day in the heat. B-b-but my b-b-b-boss is very n-n-nice. And I d-d-d-don't have to deal w-w-with the p-p-public."

Eva raised her eyebrows. "You don't like dealing with the public?"

Once again Jolissa's cheeks flamed. She hung her head, pretending to look at Mario as she petted him. "N-n-not r-r-really."

"Why is that, *mija*? You are so pretty and smart. You should do very well working with the public. Why would you not want to do that?"

Jolissa shook her head and lifted her eyes to meet Eva's. "It's th-th-the way I t-t-talk." She dropped her eyes again and waited.

"I see. Have you . . . always had a problem with stuttering?"

Jolissa lifted her eyebrows and her head simultaneously. "I . . . I g-g-guess so. I c-c-can't remember n-n-not s-s-s-stuttering."

Eva nodded and smiled. "Well, *mija*, we have time before we need to go to church. Shall I get the quilt and tell you a bit more about the queen of gospel songs's life?"

"Y-y-yes, please. Th-th-that would be n-n-nice."

✳ ✳ ✳

THE PATCH EVA POINTED OUT to Jolissa when she rejoined her on the patio showed a writing quill, and Jolissa was pleased that she was about to hear more about Fanny Crosby's song-writing career. Had it really started so early, while she was yet a teenager in school? Jolissa had trouble processing that. She remembered her own teen years as being miserable at best— trying hard not to speak in front of people, and then dreading heading home to hear her *tio* call her *idiota*—and never, *never* inviting anyone over. At least the queen of gospel songs had a loving family, encouraging her to do her best regardless of the circumstances. Jolissa couldn't help but wonder how different her life might have been if only her parents hadn't died.

But they did, she reminded herself, *so stop dreaming about the impossible. Your life is what it is, and there's nothing you can do to change it.*

"Before I tell you about some of Fanny's early writing opportunities while she was still a student at the school for the blind, I should tell you that she had some heartache to deal with."

Jolissa raised her head and fine-tuned her hearing. More heartache? She'd already lost her father and had to learn to navigate a frightening world without the capacity to see. What else could have happened to her? Surely her mother didn't die too!

"In 1838, just three years after Fanny became a student at the New York Institute for the Blind, her mother remarried, eventually producing three siblings for Fanny. But a few years later, in 1844, Fanny's stepfather abandoned the family, and once again her mother was a single parent and had to go to work to support her brood. If Fanny hadn't been in a state-financed school, the family would never have been able to afford to keep her there."

Jolissa winced at the thought. To have one husband die and your only child blinded as an infant, then remarrying and having three more children, only to be left to raise them alone must have been extremely difficult. For a brief moment Jolissa identified with Fanny's mother, recognizing a shared grief and hardship, though their lives were quite different.

"One particular incident at the school, which happened when Fanny was twenty, deeply affected Fanny's life—for years to come. She met another blind student named Alexander Van Alstyne, who loved music and thoroughly enjoyed Fanny's poetry." Eva's eyes took on a dreamy look, and she smiled as if in memory. "Young love. It knows no bounds, *mija*—not physical challenges or financial status . . ."

Her voice drifted off, and Jolissa watched her *abuela*'s face change, as if she had gone back in time. Was it possible? Could someone turn back the clock with their memories?

Eva seemed to pull herself back then, and Jolissa realized the old woman's face hadn't really changed at all. But something—some very special memory—had taken her back in time, at least for a moment.

Abuela smiled at Jolissa as if she had just remembered she was there. "I'm sorry, *mija*. The story of Fanny and Alexander's romance took me back to my own true love, Guillermo. We married when we were younger than you are now. Did I tell you that already?"

Jolissa shook her head no.

"I was seventeen, and Guillermo was twenty. Most people said we were too young, just children, really. But we knew we loved each other, and that was all that mattered. We had very little money, but we never regretted our decision." She glanced toward the house and around the yard before returning her attention to Jolissa. "It took us many years of hard work and saving to buy this little house, but we had so many happy years here, raising our children together, watching them graduate and marry and start lives of their own." Her smile faded and she sighed. "Now it's just me. Guillermo has gone on to heaven ahead of me, and my children and grandchildren are too busy to visit very often." She reached across the small table between them and laid her hand on Jolissa's arm. "But now I have you. I am so grateful that God has brought you to me, *mija*."

Not half as grateful as I am. The thought startled her. She knew she was grateful for having met her new *abuela*, but until now she had not considered to whom she was grateful. *God. I am grateful to God for* Abuela. *Yes, it's true.*

"Anyway," Eva said, interrupting Jolissa's thoughts, "enough about me. Let's get back to Fanny. As I said, she met Alexander, who so appreciated her poems and encouraged her to keep writing them. They fell in love and spent countless hours together. Alexander eventually began putting some of Fanny's poems to music. It was the perfect match!"

Jolissa imagined it was. And since they were both blind, she expected their blindness was a nonissue between them.

Eva pulled from her pocket the small book about Fanny Crosby that she'd read from once before. "Would you like to hear what Fanny said about the love she and Alexander shared?"

"Y-y-yes, I really w-w-w-would."

Abuela opened the book and flipped a few pages until she found the right spot. "These are Fanny's actual words," she explained, sliding her glasses down her nose and looking over the top of them, "written in her delightful, lilting style. Of course, because of her blindness she didn't actually pen the words, but she dictated them to others. 'From that hour two lives looked on a new universe, for love met love and all the world was changed. We were no longer blind, for the light of love showed where the lilies bloomed, and where the crystal waters found the moss-mantled spring.'" Eva looked up from her reading and pushed her glasses back into place. "Isn't that absolutely beautiful?"

Tear pricks surprised Jolissa, and she nodded. Though she'd never experienced such love and doubted very much that she ever would, she realized as she heard the words how deeply she longed to feel the same thing one day. Another desire that would no doubt die in her heart, and it hurt her even now to think about it.

"D-d-did they g-g-get m-m-m-married?" Jolissa dared to ask.

"They certainly did—and happily so, according to most accounts. They both became teachers at the institute where they'd received their own educations and where they'd met, and their friendship and romance continued. They married in 1858. Fanny was thirty-seven by then, so as you can see, they didn't rush into anything."

Eva chuckled, and so did Jolissa. She had to admit that seventeen years was quite a long time to wait for marriage. "D-d-did they h-h-have any ch-ch-children?"

Her *abuela*'s smile faded, and she slowly nodded her head. "Just one. A little girl, whom they adored. But she died as an infant, and they were devastated. Many people think her daughter's death inspired Fanny to write one of her most famous hymns, 'Safe in the Arms of Jesus.' Have you ever heard it, *mija*?"

Jolissa shook her head no.

Eva cleared her throat and then opened her mouth and sang. "'Safe in the arms of Jesus, safe on His gentle breast, there by His love o'ershaded, sweetly my soul doth rest.'" She stopped, appearing embarrassed. "My voice isn't what it used to be. But that's the refrain, and it captures the heart of the hymn. It has become one of her best-known compositions, and it was even sung in 1885 when Ulysses S. Grant was laid to rest on the banks of the Hudson River."

"R-r-really? The song was p-p-played f-f-for a President? She m-m-must have b-b-b-been very f-f-famous even th-th-then."

"Next time I'll tell you about a few of the very famous people she met in her life, not to mention some of the stunning places where she recited her poetry." She set the book down on top of the quilt, which still lay in her lap. "But now I think we'd better go inside and find something to eat before it's time to leave for church."

Jolissa hadn't realized until that moment how hungry she was. Now the thought of food beckoned, and she was ready to follow her *abuela* inside. As she started to stand, Mario hopped off her lap and stretched, yawning as he too headed inside the house, no doubt looking for his own supper.

❋ ❋ ❋

IT HAD COOLED A BIT by the time they left Eva's house to walk the two short blocks to church. *Abuela* had offered her a sweater before they left, but Jolissa insisted she didn't need one. Now she wasn't so sure.

"I've noticed you walk everywhere," Eva observed. "Don't you or your *tio* have a car?"

Jolissa felt the heat of shame creep up her neck once again. Sometimes she thought she was used to being poor and it didn't bother her anymore; other times she realized it bothered her more than she wanted to admit. Not having a car in Southern California was nearly unheard of. Of course, even if her *tio* had one, he would never have let her use it.

Jolissa realized Eva was waiting for an answer. She cleared her throat. "I d-d-don't have a car, and n-n-neither does my *t-t-tio*. He c-c-can't d-d-drive anymore, ever s-s-since his accident, and h-h-h-he s-s-said I d-d-don't need one."

There was a pause before Eva responded. "I see. Do you know how to drive?"

Jolissa breathed a sigh of relief. At least she could answer this question positively—for all the good it would do.

"Y-y-yes. I t-t-took driver t-t-training in s-s-school."

"That's good, *mija*. That was smart of you to plan ahead. You may not have a car now, but things can change."

Not in my lifetime.

A siren wailed nearby, and Jolissa shivered. Was it just from the cool evening air, or was something wrong?

She shook off the thought and turned the corner. The church came into view at the same time she heard faint strains of lively music drifting toward her, and she suddenly found herself wishing she'd brought her Bible along. Eva carried hers, and the handful of people she saw approaching the church building all seemed to have one as well. Second thoughts about going inside began to gnaw at her stomach. She shouldn't have come. She would be out of place. People would know she didn't belong there. And besides, what if they spoke to her?

Eva looped her free arm through Jolissa's, her Bible resting in the other. "I'm so pleased you've come with me, *mija*. I believe God has led you here."

The fear that had nearly overtaken her began to melt, and though she continued to grapple with insecurity, she climbed the steps to the front door of the Light House and walked inside, hanging close to Eva and wishing she were invisible.

The music she'd heard as she approached the building now echoed throughout the sanctuary, stirring up mixed emotions for Jolissa. The cheerful song, though she had never heard it before, almost made her want to dance. Of course, she would never do such a thing, particularly in church, but she was surprised that the music wasn't more somber. She also wondered if it wasn't in some way a bit disrespectful. Then again, how did she know what was appropriate or inappropriate in church? Her memories of attending with her parents were vague, though she had to admit that cheerful music didn't seem at all out of place in the context of those memories.

Since her parents died, however, she'd had little opportunity to attend church. Her *tio* cursed God for allowing him to end up in a wheelchair, and the only times he'd taken her to church over the years was for two funerals. And there certainly were no lively songs being played at those events.

Eva leaned toward her and asked in a loud whisper, "Where would you like to sit?"

Relief washed over her. She had feared her *abuela* might want to sit up front where it seemed most everyone else had gathered. She knew it would be awkward to suggest they sit in the very back row, though that would have been her preference.

Jolissa took stock of the sparse congregation. Somehow she had expected more of a crowd. Forty, perhaps fifty, people were scattered throughout the front eight or nine rows. Maybe they could compromise and at least sit a row or two behind everyone else.

She stopped and nodded toward an empty pew. Only an elderly couple sat in the row in front of it. "Would this be all right?"

Eva smiled. "This is perfect, *mija*."

Jolissa moved far enough into the pew that Eva would have room at the end by the center aisle. Jolissa sat close, on her left. As the music continued, it occurred to Jolissa that her *abuela* no doubt knew many of the people in that room. If Jolissa hadn't been with her, she probably would have sat up front with her friends. That she hadn't pushed to do that caused Jolissa's heart to swell with gratitude. What a kind and thoughtful woman her *abuela* was! Jolissa smiled to herself. Yes, she was grateful indeed that God had brought them together.

Chapter 13

THOUGH SHE'D DONE IT FOR YEARS, walking alone in the dark usually unnerved Jolissa. Not tonight. All she could think of was how quickly the church service had flown by. She was shocked to realize she could have stayed and listened to the teaching all night, even if she had understood little of it.

I understood the part about the children, though, she thought as she hurried down the sidewalk, having walked *Abuela* home before heading home herself. *The minister was talking about the same part of the Bible I read the other night, in that book called Mark, about Jesus and the things that mattered to Him when He was here on earth. Whatever else I didn't understand, I got that part. Jesus cared about children and said we should be like them if we wanted to get into heaven. I'm just not sure how to do that.*

For the first time since she'd left the church, she noticed the cool temperatures and shivered, speeding up her pace a bit. She would have to remember that the heat wave was over and bring a sweater with her next time.

Next time. How can there be a next time if I have to skip class to go to church? Of course, I could go on Sunday instead . . .

Her thoughts trailed off as she noticed the flashing red lights across the street. Police cars—two of them—parked in front of the house where the little girl with the sad eyes lived. Jolissa's heart skipped a beat at the thought that something might have happened to her. *Please, God, let her be all right! Take care of her, please!*

There she was, praying again, but she realized she meant it with all her heart. She could only hope that an almighty God would honor the request of someone like her—if not for her sake, then for the child's.

She slowed her pace, straining to see something—anything that would give her a clue about what was going on. She came to a tree and stopped, watching as her heart thumped against her chest. At last a policeman emerged from the front door, his hand firmly grasping the arm of a heavyset man in a dirty T-shirt and sweatpants. He was barefoot, and his hands were cuffed behind him.

It wasn't the first time Jolissa had seen such a thing in the older neighborhood where she lived and worked, but this time the scene held her attention. Who was the man? The little girl's father? The age seemed right. But where was the child?

She watched as the officer escorted the man to the black-and-white cruiser and then carefully placed him in the backseat. Another officer came out of the house, followed by the woman Jolissa had seen there before. The woman was carrying the little girl, whose head was buried in the woman's shoulder. The child appeared to be crying.

Oh, mijita, *what happened in there? What have you seen? What have you been through tonight?*

Jolissa stayed in her spot until the police car drove away, and the woman and child returned inside the house. Her heart heavy, she turned toward home.

✳ ✳ ✳

THOUGH JOSEPH YELLED AT HER when she came in, she ignored him and went straight to her room. With no lock to keep him out, she closed the door and pushed her small dresser in front of it. Her heart raced at the chance she was taking, but she couldn't bear to face him that night. Let him rant outside her door; she would ignore him until he gave up.

She flopped on her bed, allowing her mind to drift to an imaginary world where her parents had never died and where even her grandmother still lived. It was a world she hadn't visited in a while, telling herself she was too old for that sort of nonsense. But this night she needed such a retreat. Though the evening had started well with her visit to *Abuela*'s house and then the service at church, all her warm feelings had faded the moment she saw the police cars in front of the little girl's house. She'd known there was something wrong there, from the moment she first spotted the child. But she was such a coward she had ignored the girl's sad eyes and silent cries. Jolissa had done nothing to help, and now look what had happened.

But what else could I have done? I have no right to go to their home when I don't even know them. They would have thrown me out, maybe even called the cops. Then what?

Her memory went then to *Tio*'s threat some years earlier, when he'd warned her that if she ever got arrested she could rot in jail because he wasn't about to come and bail her out. She'd never even come close to being arrested because she was so careful to obey all the laws, refusing even to jaywalk on a quiet street. But now, a child was obviously in danger. She was sure of it, but what was she to do?

Abuela. *I must talk with her about this tomorrow. She'll know what to do. She'll find a way to help. Oh, if only I lived with you,* Abuela, *and not here with my* Tio *who hates me. God, why? Why must I live here with this man? And why must a little child suffer so? The Bible tells of Jesus holding children on His lap, of caring for them and telling others they should be like them. Help me to understand this, God. Nothing makes sense to me right now. Nothing!*

She rolled over onto her stomach then and let the tears flow into her pillow.

❋ ❋ ❋

Jolissa woke early the next morning and left breakfast on the table for her *tio* before he was awake. Then she hurried from the house, her heart racing as she neared the spot where the man had been hauled away in the police car the night before. Once again she stopped and watched from behind the tree.

Why? What do I expect to see? It's too early for the child to be outside.

Yet she couldn't force herself to walk away. Besides, she had plenty of time before she had to be at work. And the pull on her heart toward the little girl was just too strong to ignore.

Help her, God. Please help her!

"Look at that woman hiding behind the tree!"

The taunting voice and muffled giggles caught her attention. She turned to see three preteen boys, all with backpacks, heading in her direction, most likely on their way to school. Her cheeks flamed, and she couldn't think of anything to say to explain her actions.

The tallest of the group, no doubt the leader of the pack, smirked. "What are you doing? Spying?"

The boys all guffawed in response, though the smallest boy, who had a sprinkling of freckles across his nose, seemed less enthusiastic than the others.

"I . . . I w-w-w-was j-j-just—"

The ringleader interrupted her with a whoop of delight. "Check it out! She can't talk! No wonder she was hiding." He squinted his eyes and leaned his head toward her.

"Wh-wh-why d-d-d-don't y-y-you t-t-take s-s-some s-s-speech l-l-lessons, d-d-dummy?"

The boys roared with laughter and passed on by, poking and jabbing one another as they continued to toss insults back and forth. Tears stung her eyes, but she couldn't look away. Just before turning the corner, the small boy with the freckles looked back. He wasn't laughing. When their eyes met, he quickly looked away and ran to catch up with his friends.

Dummy. Idiota. The names echoed in her ears. How could she ever expect to help someone like the little girl with the sad eyes when she couldn't even help herself? Who was she kidding? What good was it for her to go to school and pretend that she would one day be a social worker? Living with her *tio* and working at the cleaners was the best she could ever hope for.

Her head drooped and her shoulders sagged as she turned from the tree and placed one leaden foot in front of the other on her way to work. She'd be early, but Mr. Peterson wouldn't mind. He was always happy to have her come in early or even stay a bit late, so long as she didn't expect extra pay.

Wiping tears from her eyes, she pressed on until she came within sight of the Evergreen Laundry and Dry Cleaners sign. Then she took a moment to pull herself together before heading inside.

Chapter 14

EVA HAD SPENT MUCH OF THE MORNING IN PRAYER, reading from the Scriptures and listening for God's direction. She didn't want to make this decision lightly; she had to be certain it was the Lord's will before she said a word.

By the time lunchtime rolled around, she had no doubt. Her heart soared with anticipation as she fixed herself a bowl of tomato soup and then sat at the table and ate it while Mario rubbed against her leg and meowed for attention.

"You miss your new friend, don't you?" She reached down and stroked him, and he arched his back in approval. "Maybe she'll stop by this afternoon. I know she enjoyed the service last night." She straightened back up and took another spoonful of soup. Yes, she was sure of it. Jolissa had indeed enjoyed the service, and Eva sensed she would come back to church again. God was up to something in that young woman's life.

She finished her soup and got up to carry the bowl to the sink. Should she have a couple of cookies for dessert? She smiled. No, she would wait and see if Jolissa came over after work. Then they could have cookies together.

She washed the handful of dishes in the sink and set them in the drainer, checked to be sure Mario had food and water, and then went outside to enjoy the early afternoon sunshine. The cat followed her and hopped onto her lap the minute she was situated in the redwood chair.

"It's beautiful out here today, isn't it? The sun is already warming your fur."

She leaned her head back and closed her eyes, the sounds of Mario's purring and an occasional chirping bird fading into the distance as she drifted off.

"*Abuela*? Are y-y-you home?"

The faint voice cut into her slumber, and she pulled herself back from a forgotten dream. "Jolissa? *Mija*, is that you?"

"I'm h-h-here. J-j-just outside the f-f-fence."

Mario leapt from her lap, and Eva stood up and walked toward the gate, which she always kept locked from the inside.

"*Mija*, I'm so glad you've come!" She unlocked the gate and pulled it open. "Mario and I were just taking a nap in the sunshine."

Jolissa's eyes widened. "I sh-sh-shouldn't have b-b-bothered y-y-you. I r-r-rang the d-d-d-doorbell, b-b-but you didn't answer s-s-so I thought y-y-you m-m-might be out h-h-here."

"You haven't bothered me at all," Eva insisted, ushering her into the yard and closing the gate behind her. "Mario and I have been hoping you would come. Do you want to sit out here for a while, or would you rather go inside?"

The young woman shook her head. "Th-th-this is f-f-fine."

"Have you eaten?"

"I had a s-s-sandwich for l-l-lunch b-b-before I c-c-came."

"Perfect." Abuela smiled and indicated a chair. "Sit down, *mija*. I've been waiting to have dessert until you got here. I'll get some cookies and lemonade while you keep Mario company. He's missed you."

Humming "Blessed Assurance, Jesus Is Mine" Eva headed into the house, her heart nearly bursting with joy that Jolissa had come—and that God had given Eva the green light to share some news with her.

IF ABUELA ONLY KNEW how close I came to not stopping by here at all. She scratched the top of Mario's head and cuddled him close as they waited for Eva to return. Jolissa had worked straight through her break in an attempt to block out the mocking words of the boys who had caught her behind the tree, watching the little girl's house. As she sat in the park after work, eating her sandwich, she'd nearly convinced herself not to go to her *abuela*'s again so soon, thinking she might be making a pest of herself. But the thought of going home to face *Tío* was more than she was up to in her already fragile state. And so she had ended up at Eva's home, heartbroken when the old woman didn't answer the door but pleased that she'd had the nerve to call out to her in case she was in the backyard.

And now, here I am, petting a cat that isn't mine, sitting in a chair in a yard behind a house that isn't mine, trying to find comfort from being with a grandmother who isn't really mine either. But what else do I have?

"Here you are, *mija*." Eva appeared carrying a small tray with a plate of cookies and two glasses. "The pitcher of lemonade is in the refrigerator. Would you mind getting it? And why don't you get the singing quilt from my bed while you're in there? Maybe we'll have time for another story while you're here. You're not in a hurry to leave, are you?"

Jolissa shook her head. She was in no hurry whatsoever.

She let herself into the house and went to Eva's bedroom to retrieve the quilt first. Carrying it carefully tucked under one arm, she stopped in the kitchen and got the lemonade from the refrigerator, all the time wondering at why this sweet woman would trust someone like her to walk freely through her home.

Once outside she handed Eva the quilt and then poured the lemonade. Mario had appeared more than slightly disgruntled when she moved him off her lap before going into the house, but he quickly resettled there when she returned.

"So," Eva said as she set her glass down on the small table between them, "you said last night that you enjoyed the service. What do you think today, now that you've had time to think about it a little more?"

Jolissa didn't want to tell her that she really hadn't had nearly as much time as she would have liked to focus on church because of all that had happened since she dropped her off the evening before. But there was no need to worry her with all that.

"I l-l-liked it very m-m-m-much."

"And will you come back with me again?"

Jolissa paused. "Y-y-yes. B-b-but it m-m-might have to b-b-be on S-S-Sunday instead of W-W-Wednesday because I c-c-can't m-m-miss too much s-s-school."

Eva nodded. "Of course you can't. You need to finish your studies so you can become a social worker." She leaned toward her. "And you will be a wonderful social worker, *mija*. You have a sharp mind and a very kind heart."

Jolissa raised her eyebrows. "I d-d-do? You r-r-really th-th-think so?"

Eva's smile was warm. "Of course I do. Why, anyone who knows you would see that right away."

Idiota! The word echoed in her mind, but she pushed it away. She wanted so desperately to believe her *abuela* instead. "I r-r-really w-w-want to be a s-s-social w-w-worker, b-b-but sometimes I th-th-think I c-c-can't because I c-c-can't t-t-talk right."

Abuela reached toward her and laid her hand on her arm. "Oh, *mija*, you can be anything God calls you to be. And I believe He has put this desire in your heart. Don't let fear stop you. Keep pursuing your dreams! Go to school, study hard, but most of all, pray and get close to God." She paused. "He is calling you. You hear Him, don't you?"

Jolissa frowned. She hadn't heard any voices, and yet she somehow knew her *abuela* was right. God was calling her. She just wished she knew how to answer.

"I . . . I th-th-think so." She nodded slightly. "Y-y-yes. I h-h-hear Him."

Eva's smile lit up her eyes. "I knew it. I knew it! *Sí, mija*, He is calling you, and I am excited to see what will come of it all. He has wonderful plans for you, I promise."

Jolissa hesitated. Wonderful plans. For someone like her? It was almost too much to imagine, let alone hope for.

"*Abuela* . . ." Jolissa took a deep breath, fighting tears but unable to stop herself, despite her previous decision not to burden Eva with the news. "S-s-s-something happened l-l-last night—after I l-l-left here. Something b-b-bad."

Eva's expression grew serious. "Tell me about it, *mija*."

And so she did. She told of the police cars, of the man in handcuffs, of the little girl crying on the older woman's shoulder. She told about locking herself in her room so she wouldn't have to deal with her *tio* that night, and then leaving early that morning before he was up. She even told about the boys who made fun of her. By the time she was through, Eva had handed her a couple of tissues, and Jolissa was mopping her face.

"I'm s-s-sorry, *Abuela*. I d-d-didn't mean t-t-to—"

Eva patted her arm. "Don't apologize. You are safe here. You can tell me anything you wish. And you can cry too, if you need to." She shook her head. "So much to carry on your shoulders. Very soon you will have to turn it all over to Jesus and let Him carry it. Are you ready to do that now?"

Jolissa's heart raced. She longed to say yes, but the word wouldn't move past the lump in her throat. After a few deep breaths, she said, "M-m-maybe later. W-w-would you t-t-tell me m-m-more about the s-s-singing quilt first?"

Eva smiled, but Jolissa thought she saw a tinge of sadness in it. "Of course, *mija*. I will do that now."

Jolissa felt her shoulders relax, and she leaned back in her chair to listen.

* * *

EVA LIFTED THE QUILT FROM HER LAP, even as she wrestled with her disappointment. She had so hoped that Jolissa was ready to make a commitment to Christ, but just as the young woman asked to hear more of the quilt story instead, Eva had sensed God saying, "Not quite yet . . . but soon." And so she had backed off.

She pointed to a design that appeared to be a small wooden stage with a microphone on a stand. "This stage and microphone represent the next step in Fanny's illustrious life. It wasn't enough that this sightless woman wrote poetry and that much of it was put to music; she was also called to speak and to recite her poetry on many occasions."

Eva laid the quilt back in her lap. It was obvious Jolissa was paying close attention, though she continued to stroke Mario, who purred his appreciation.

"In 1843 Fanny joined a group of lobbyists in Washington. Their goal was to push for more and better educational opportunities for the blind. As it turned out, Fanny got the privilege of reciting one of her poems in the US Senate."

Eva closed her eyes and spoke from memory.

"O ye who here from every state convene,
Illustrious band, may we not hope the scene
That you now behold will prove to every mind
Instruction hath a ray to cheer the blind."

She opened her eyes and looked at Jolissa. "Can you imagine the impact she had? Sightless and only in her early twenties at the time, she was the first woman ever to speak in the US Senate. She first paid tribute to Congress and then to her Lord and Savior, speaking so sweetly of His loving care that she brought many of her listeners to tears. Then she recited another of her poems, this one calling everyone present to a deeper realization of what education could do for the blind. And wasn't she the perfect visual aid for her demonstration?"

Jolissa had to admit she was, though she couldn't imagine how anyone could stand in front of so many important people and speak to them. *Then again, she might not have been able to see but she didn't have trouble speaking—like I do.*

"Less than a year later, Fanny was part of the group from her school who gave a concert for Congress. She had written an original composition, which she recited to everyone present, this time calling for establishing schools for the blind in every state. John Quincy Adams himself heard her recitation and praised her words."

Eva paused to take a sip of lemonade before continuing. "Fanny made several appearances in places of government and became friends with several politicians and other important people of her time. She even composed a special poem in honor of President James K. Polk when he visited the school where she was now considered a graduate pupil and would soon be added to the official faculty roster."

"In s-s-some ways it w-w-was l-l-like being b-b-blind helped her."

Eva lifted her eyebrows and smiled. "Well now, you are absolutely right, *mija*. I'm glad you see how God can use what we think of as our weaknesses to accomplish things that we could never do on our own." She leaned over the little table toward Jolissa. "That's how we learn to depend on God's strength—by being obedient to step out and do things that we know we can never do in our own strength and abilities."

Jolissa didn't answer, but Eva could tell she was seriously considering this new concept. How Eva prayed it would be one more step in bringing the young woman closer to a total acceptance of Jesus as her Lord and Savior!

Chapter 15

Jolissa had scarcely been able to concentrate during her class, as her mind returned, over and over, to the incredible achievements of a blind woman named Fanny Crosby. Eva's comment about how God can use our weaknesses to accomplish things we could never do on our own rang in her ears. She sensed her *abuela*'s words held a great truth that she needed to understand, but she just couldn't quite lay hold of it.

Her heart raced as she returned home, hoping she could sneak past her *tio* and make it to her room unseen. It didn't work.

"So, you have finally come home." The statement was laced with sarcasm, and Jolissa cringed as she stopped in the doorway to the living room where he sat in his usual spot in the wheelchair in front of the TV. He had turned the chair so he could see her, his face a dark scowl.

"Are you going to lie to me about where you've been and why you left me here to take care of myself, knowing how hard that is for me?"

Jolissa knew exactly how difficult it was for her *tio* to fix his own meals, but she simply hadn't had time between her visit with *Abuela* and her class. Though she regretted not coming back to fix his dinner, she knew it would do no good to say so.

"Answer me!" His roar nearly caused her knees to buckle, but she managed to stay on her feet, though she dropped her gaze to avoid his.

"I . . . I meant t-t-t-to come and f-f-fix y-y-your dinner, T-T-Tio, b-b-but—"

"I don't want to hear your lies or excuses. I made myself a sandwich, so all I want now is for you to get out of my sight. But you'd better make sure my breakfast is waiting for me in the morning and my lunch is in the refrigerator before you go to work tomorrow. And if you're not home to fix my dinner in the evening, you can just find somewhere else to live."

Jolissa jerked her head up, feeling her eyes go wide. *Tio* would do that? He would kick her out, knowing she had nowhere to go? With only a part-time job she would never be able to afford her own place. What would happen to her then? And what would happen to *Tio* if there was no one to take care of him? Didn't he need her as much as she needed him? Surely he knew that and wouldn't do such a thing!

Joseph's eyes narrowed. "I know what you're thinking, you ungrateful girl. You think I won't throw you out because I need you. But what good are you if you're not here when I need your help?" He rolled his chair a few feet in her direction, and she took a step backward.

"You're an adult now, Jolissa. I don't need to take care of you anymore. I only let you live here because you can help me do the things I can't do myself. But if you're not going to do that, then what good are you?" He shook his head. "No good—not to me or anyone else. You are a worthless *idiota*, and I will not put up with you sponging off me any longer. Do you understand?"

How her heart cried out to remind him that she gave him nearly every dime she made to cover her room and board, but she bit her tongue and pressed her lips together, nodding her head to let him know she understood.

"What's that? Are you admitting that you understand what I'm telling you? Is a nod the best you can do?" He smirked. "I suppose it is easier than trying to talk when you can't even do that right."

Again, she remained quiet, wanting nothing more than to run to her room and hide away until morning. At last he sneered, "Go on. Get out of my sight. But don't forget what I said about my meals. I better not have to fix them for myself ever again."

With a final nod, she turned and disappeared into her room, sobbing as she threw herself across the bed. Fanny Crosby might have been blind, but Jolissa thought that couldn't have been nearly as difficult as what she had to endure, because at least Fanny knew she was loved.

✳ ✳ ✳

THROUGHOUT THE NIGHT Eva wrestled with sleep, tossing and turning, almost drifting off and then jerking back awake by some unknown thought or whisper. At last she gave up and pulled herself from bed.

Maybe a cup of warm milk will help. Mama always swore by it, and Mario certainly loves it.

She fixed enough to pour a little in her pet's bowl. Mario, who had followed her to the kitchen, meowed his gratitude and immediately began lapping up his treat. Eva used the rest of the warm liquid to fill a mug, which she took with her to her favorite prayer spot. Settling in the old rocker in her bedroom, she placed the cup on the nightstand between the chair and her bed, then covered her knees with the afghan that lay across the rocker's arm. There was no doubt that her Lord would meet her there because she knew it was He who had called her to come.

"I'm here, Father," she whispered. "Speak to me. Is this about Jolissa?"

The affirmation rang in her heart, and she nodded. Just as she'd suspected. With a sigh of anticipation, she closed her eyes and began to pray. She would stay as long as it took to be sure her Father had released her to go back to bed.

✳   ✳   ✳

WITH *TIO*'S BREAKFAST ON THE TABLE and his lunch in the refrigerator, Jolissa snagged her backpack and slipped out the door before her uncle emerged from his room. She didn't have to be at work for a couple of hours, so she headed straight for her *abuela*'s house. She wasn't even sure why she felt such a need to see her and talk with her, but the desire had built in her throughout the night. She hoped she wouldn't wake the old woman, but she'd been afraid to take the chance to call her first. The last thing she wanted was for her uncle to come into the kitchen and catch her on the phone.

Relief flooded her heart when *Abuela* opened after her first knock. At least she hadn't wakened her!

"I'm s-s-sorry," she said immediately, "b-b-but I need to t-t-talk to y-y-you, and I couldn't w-w-wait until th-th-this afternoon b-b-because I h-h-h-have to g-g-get h-h-home to f-f-fix *T-T-Tio*'s dinner and—"

"*Calmate, mija*. Calm down." Eva took Jolissa's arm and drew her inside. "There is no need to explain. I've been waiting for you. I even made a pot of coffee. Come, let's go into the kitchen and sit down."

Too stunned to speak, Jolissa followed Eva into the kitchen.

"Look, *mija*. Even Mario is waiting for you."

The cat lay curled up on a chair at the table, but he raised his head when they walked in.

"I d-d-don't unders-s-stand." Jolissa frowned. "H-h-how did y-y-you know?"

Abuela smiled as she poured coffee into two mugs and set them on the table. "I've been praying for you. *El Señor* told me you were coming."

El Señor. Jolissa hadn't spent much time in church since her parents died, but enough that she knew her *abuela* was referring to God. But the concept that He spoke to Eva about her was too much to grasp.

She shook her head. "I d-d-don't understand," she repeated. "Wh-wh-why were y-y-you praying f-f-f-for me? And why w-w-would God s-s-speak to you about m-m-m-me?"

Eva smiled. "Sit down and I will tell you. Cream or sugar?"

Jolissa frowned. Cream or sugar? Oh, the coffee! She shook her head. "N-n-no, thank you. J-j-just black is f-f-f-fine." She lifted Mario from the chair and sat down, allowing the cat to resettle in her lap.

"I know it has been a long night for you, *mija*." Eva laid her hand on Jolissa's arm. "Are you ready to tell me about it?" She paused. "All of it?"

Tears pricked Jolissa's eyes. She was so tired of keeping everything inside, but speaking was such a strain for her. This time the need to pour out her heart won the battle, and she started with telling Eva everything about her life that she could remember—good, bad, and otherwise, though most of it bad. She ended up back at what she'd seen at the little girl's home on Wednesday evening, the boys who had taunted her the next morning, and finishing with her *tio*'s threat the night before. By the time she'd finished, she felt as if she'd emptied out her entire insides. Though it was a relief, she wondered now what she would use to fill the gaping hole it had left within her.

Chapter 16

IT WAS ALL JOLISSA COULD DO to stay away from her *abuela*'s house after work, but she knew she needed to go home and spend some time making a special dinner for *Tío* before heading to class. But the next morning, with no work or school on Saturday, she scooted out the front door as soon as her uncle's breakfast and lunch were prepared and waiting for him. The warm welcome she received, both from Eva and Mario, made her heart soar with hope.

Why? Why do I feel hopeful when nothing has changed . . . except that I finally told Abuela *all the things that were breaking my heart? This time I know I didn't hold anything back—at least, nothing I can remember.*

She sat on one end of the sofa, with Mario once again curled up on her lap. *Abuela* had gone to retrieve the quilt, and Jolissa waited anxiously, as if she expected more than just another installment of Fanny Crosby's story.

Eva's smile was warm as she returned to the room, the quilt folded over her arm and the small book about Fanny Crosby in her hand. "I am so glad that we have come to my favorite square on the singing quilt." She sat down at the opposite end of the couch, then opened the quilt and laid it out between them. "Do you see this patch, *mija*?"

She pointed to the very center of the quilt, where a simple brown cross held an obvious place of honor.

Jolissa nodded, sensing there was a deep significance to the particular patch.

"I love this part of the story." Eva closed her eyes briefly and sighed before returning her gaze to Jolissa. "Without it, there would be no story—no singing quilt, no queen of gospel songs named Fanny Crosby. And we wouldn't be sitting here having this conversation."

Jolissa raised her eyebrows and nodded, eager for *Abuela* to continue.

"As I've already told you, Fanny's grandmother had a great influence on the young girl, teaching her the Scriptures and the importance of prayer." She leaned forward as if to emphasize her point. "But no one gets into heaven on someone else's faith. It must become personal."

Personal. Jolissa was certain that her *abuela* was trying to convey more than something that happened to Fanny Crosby. She determined to listen carefully.

"This dear young woman had published her first book at the age of twenty-four, met famous people, recited her poems in Congress . . . but there was something missing."

"You m-m-mean because she c-c-c-couldn't s-s-see?"

Eva smiled. "In a way, yes. But it wasn't her lack of physical sight that was the real issue. It was her lack of spiritual sight."

Jolissa frowned. "I d-d-d-don't unders-s-stand. She w-w-was r-r-raised as a Christian, r-r-right?"

Abuela hesitated. "Yes . . . and no." She laid her hand on Jolissa's arm. "Have you ever heard that old saying, 'You can lead a horse to water but you can't make it drink?'"

Jolissa nodded, though she couldn't imagine what it had to do with Fanny Crosby's story.

"That's the way it is with faith. Fanny's grandmother could take her to church, teach her the Scriptures, pray with her, but she couldn't make her granddaughter's faith real or personal. Fanny had to make that decision for herself."

Personal. Jolissa thought the story was beginning to feel more that way all the time. "S-s-so, what h-h-h-happened?"

"Why don't I let Fanny tell you in her own words?" Eva set the quilt down and picked up the book she'd read from before. She opened to a marked page, and Jolissa realized her *abuela* had already planned on reading this specific part of the book to her.

"Before I read Fanny's words about her conversion experience, I want to lay a little groundwork first. I've already told you that Fanny's mother and especially her grandmother modeled and taught their faith to Fanny, but throughout her years at the school she was required to participate in daily morning and evening prayers. The students also attended services on Sunday morning and evening, so the foundation had been laid. But still her faith had not become personal.

"Then, in 1849, a cholera epidemic struck New York City, and Fanny volunteered to help nurse the sick. Being around so much sickness and death really impacted her. People who knew her said it made her more introspective, more concerned with the welfare of her soul. Though she was already deeply involved with social, political, and educational reform, she realized for the first time that she didn't truly love God. And how could she? She knew quite a bit *about* Him, but she didn't really *know* Him."

"B-b-but He's God. H-h-how c-c-could anyone actually know H-H-Him?"

Eva smiled. "I was hoping you'd ask. With Fanny now concerned with the state of her eternal soul, she was truly ready for the revival meetings that were held at a nearby church when she was thirty-one."

Jolissa was surprised. She was still used to thinking of Fanny as a child, but a thirty-one-year-old adult, still searching for a personal faith? The woman was ten years older than Jolissa, so maybe there was still hope for her after all.

Abuela smiled. "This is where the cross comes in— as it must if faith is to become personal to anyone. Fanny attended those revival meetings, even going forward to pray after two of them. But still her soul felt empty."

Empty. Like me, since I poured out my heart to Abuela *yesterday.*

Eva looked down at the open book in her lap and began reading what Fanny wrote about the third revival meeting. "After a prayer was offered, they began to sing the grand old consecration hymn, 'Alas, and Did My Savior Bleed,' and when they reached the third line of the fifth stanza, 'Here, Lord, I give myself away,' my very soul was flooded with celestial light. I sprang to my feet, shouting, 'Hallelujah'"

Abuela lifted her head and fixed her watery eyes on Jolissa. "Fanny's faith had at last become personal. Though she later admitted that she had a lot of spiritual growing up to do, she had at last graduated from her mother's and grandmother's faith to her own. And that's what made all the difference."

Tears stung Jolissa's eyes, but she didn't even try to blink them back or brush them away. They spilled over onto her cheeks and dripped down onto her lap.

"You want that sort of personal faith too, don't you, *mija*?"

Jolissa nodded, not trusting herself to speak.

Abuela took Jolissa's hands in hers. "Do you believe that Jesus is the Son of God?"

Jolissa nodded again. She believed it more at that moment than she ever had before.

"And do you believe that He loves you so much that He died for you on the Cross to pay the price for your sins?"

Jolissa's heart felt as if it would burst with the pain of her own sins. Why had she never realized their depth before this moment? "Y-y-yes."

Eva's face softened. "Would you like to ask Him to forgive you and to be your Lord and your Savior, to send His Spirit to live inside you?"

There was nothing Jolissa wanted more, but again all she could do was nod, knowing her *abuela* somehow understood what she was feeling.

"Close your eyes, *mija*. We will talk to God about this together."

With her eyes closed and her heart pounding in her ears, Jolissa listened as her *abuela* first asked God to help Jolissa yield her life to Him, and then spoke directly to Jolissa. "Just tell Him what's in your heart, *mija*. He will understand."

Jolissa hesitated but knew she could not pass up this moment. It seemed so . . . eternal, so permanent and powerful. She didn't want to miss it.

"I w-w-want to know Y-Y-You . . . p-personally. L-l-like F-F-Fanny C-C-Crosby and m-m-my *abuela*. Please f-f-f-forgive me. Please be m-m-my S-S-Savior and L-L-Lord."

Peace and joy, like waves of warm honey, washed over her, filling her heart to overflowing, even as the tears continued to flow down her cheeks. At that moment her question of how she would fill the emptiness within her was answered, and she knew she would never be the same.

* * *

JOLISSA FELT AS IF HER FEET didn't touch the ground for the rest of the day. Even when she forced herself to leave her *abuela*'s house to go home in plenty of time to fix dinner for her *tio*, her heart continued to soar.

"It's about time you came back." The gruff statement was her greeting when she stepped into the living room and saw her uncle in his usual spot in front of the TV, an old western flickering across the screen. His back was to her. "Where have you been all day?"

She smiled, though she knew he couldn't see it. "I w-w-was visiting w-w-with . . ." She paused. If she said she was with her *abuela*, he would accuse her of lying. No sense agitating him anymore than necessary. "A f-f-friend."

He snorted. "Ha! Who would be a friend to someone like you?"

The dart that usually pierced her heart fell short, as she realized she now had a Friend who was with her no matter where she went or what she was doing. She decided not to take her *tio*'s bait.

"I got a chicken out of the freezer this morning," she commented as she walked past him into the kitchen. "I'm going to start it now so it will be done in time for dinner."

The old man snorted again but made no comment.

By the time the chicken was frying and she was ready to start the salad, she could hear her uncle snoring as he sat in his wheelchair. She looked at him through the doorway and realized how difficult it must be for him to spend his entire life confined to that chair. Her heart squeezed to think she'd never truly considered that before.

Turning back to the task at hand, she washed the vegetables and set about cutting them up and tossing them into a large bowl. *Tio loves rice.* The thought surprised her nearly as much as her desire to fix something special for him. She didn't kid herself that he'd thank her for it, but maybe it would help make his life just a little less miserable.

Besides, I'm going to church with Abuela *tomorrow.*

She smiled. Who would have thought that just one day—one *decision*—could make such a difference? But there was no denying that it did—not only in Fanny Crosby's life but also in Jolissa Montoya's.

＊ ＊ ＊

JOLISSA WAS STUNNED at how much fuller the church was on Sunday morning than on the previous Wednesday evening. She thought she saw a couple of familiar faces from the gathering a few nights earlier, but she didn't remember any names.

Everyone knew Eva, though, which didn't surprise her at all. How could anyone not love her *abuela*? She was the kindest woman in the world, at least as far as Jolissa was concerned, and just that morning on their way to church Eva had said that she now considered herself Jolissa's "spiritual mother" because God had given her the privilege of leading her to Christ.

My spiritual mother. The corners of Jolissa's mouth tugged upward at the thought.

"You are happy, *mija?*"

Startled, Jolissa turned to Eva, who walked beside her down the center aisle toward the front of the church.

Jolissa stopped, and her *abuela* stopped with her. No doubt Eva had asked the question because Jolissa had been smiling, but yes, she was happy. Very much so.

She nodded. "Y-y-yes, *Abuela*. I am v-v-very h-h-happy."

The old woman gave a quick nod, her eyes dancing as she smiled. "As am I, *mija*. This is a wonderful day—your first time to come to church as a true believer, a born-again child of God."

A true believer. A child of God. Yes, that was her identity now. No longer was she the *idiota* orphan whose uncle despised her. God Himself had become her Father, and *Abuela* had read her a Scripture that said He was a Father to the fatherless. *That's me, but I'm not fatherless anymore.*

"Shall we sit here?" Eva indicated the partially empty row to their left, and Jolissa nodded, slipping in and scooting over to leave room for *Abuela*.

They settled in, each with a Bible on their laps. Jolissa was glad she'd remembered to bring hers when she left the house that morning, though she knew she'd need her *abuela*'s help to locate the sections the pastor would read.

In minutes the music started, and Jolissa rose to her feet with the rest of the congregation. She didn't recognize the song, though the words were visible on a screen on the front wall. She read the words as others sang them, and marveled at how she felt as she realized the song was a call to worship, an invitation to praise God.

I want to praise You, God. I want to worship You and love You. Help me learn how to do that, Lord. Teach me.

In that moment she realized that worship meant giving God her heart, all of it—good, bad, or otherwise—and allowing Him to change it as it pleased Him. Her heart, her plans, her dreams, her very life were no longer her own. Everything belonged to Him now, and she could trust Him to do what was right and best with all of it. Another wave of peace, much like she'd experienced the previous day at her *abuela*'s house, washed over her. Tears of joy stung her eyes, and the words on the screen blurred.

The remainder of the service seemed to fly by, and before she knew it the congregation was once again on its feet. Before they sang a final song, the pastor asked if anyone would like to come forward for prayer, especially anyone wanting to make a first-time commitment to Christ.

Jolissa's heart was torn. She'd made that commitment yesterday, hadn't she? And yet she felt a pull to join the handful of others walking toward the front of the church.

Eva laid a hand on her arm. "If you want to go forward, go ahead. You prayed to receive Jesus yesterday, but it's always good to make a public declaration. Besides, it will give others a chance to welcome you into the family."

She felt a stab of uncertainty at the idea of having others approach her, and yet she knew now that going forward was the right thing to do. She nodded, laid her Bible on the pew behind her, and stepped out into the aisle.

Chapter 17

"Are you sure you want to hear more about Fanny Crosby today?"

"If y-y-you d-d-don't mind t-t-telling me." Not only did Jolissa's heart feel full, but her stomach did as well. They'd come back to Eva's house after church, and Jolissa had helped her *abuela* make a salad and some sandwiches. They'd even spent some time making flan, and Jolissa was thrilled that she now knew how to make it and it had turned out so well. Now they sat out in the patio, enjoying the picture-perfect weather. Mario lay in the shade of Jolissa's chair, curled up by her feet.

Eva chuckled. "If I don't mind? Aye, *mija*, there is nothing I like better than telling you about this wonderful singing quilt." She lifted it from her lap and gazed lovingly at it before setting it back down. "And look how God has used it already."

Jolissa felt her eyes widen. God had used the quilt? Yes, of course He had! It was the story of Fanny Crosby that had helped her understand her own need for a personal faith and relationship with God, but she hadn't realized it until this moment.

She smiled. "Th-th-that's t-t-true."

Eva nodded. "Then we shall pick up where we left off yesterday. And that, *mija*, brings us right back to the cross in the middle of the quilt." Her eyes softened. "The cross must always be at the center of everything—everything! Never forget that."

Jolissa nodded. "I w-w-won't. I p-p-promise, *Abuela*."

"Good." Eva sighed. "I won't show you a new patch today then. I've already told you about the blind student she met, Alexander Van Alstyne, and how they had a very long romance. Their relationship began when Fanny was just twenty, and she was thirty-seven before they finally married. She had become a Christian during that time, as I told you yesterday, and Alexander's faith was also quite strong. And though Fanny served God admirably as a single woman, in many ways her ministry really opened up when she and Alexander married and left the school to establish their own home and family."

"Th-th-that's so r-r-romantic. B-b-but wasn't it h-h-h-hard, with b-b-both of them being b-b-blind?"

Eva smiled. "I'm sure it was. But I'm also sure that neither of them considered it extraordinarily so. After all, they were both quite used to being sightless."

"B-b-but you s-s-said their only child d-d-died. That m-m-must have been t-t-terrible."

"I can't imagine anything worse than losing a child." A cloud passed over the old woman's face, and she reached out to lay a hand on Jolissa's arm. "Except maybe losing both parents when you are still so very young."

Jolissa nodded. "But n-n-now I have a F-F-Father."

Eva's smile lit up her face. "You certainly do, *mija*. And He will never leave you or forsake you. He has promised, and He always keeps His promises."

"He will t-t-take care of m-m-me l-l-like He took c-c-care of F-F-Fanny and her h-h-husband."

"Exactly. And Fanny and Alexander understood that, even when they lost their beloved baby daughter. I told you that many believe that incident inspired one of Fanny's most famous songs, 'Safe in the Arms of Jesus,' didn't I?"

Jolissa nodded again. "I w-w-would like to h-h-hear it s-s-someday."

"And you will. The worship leader at church is a good friend of mine. I'll ask her to play it especially for you one day soon."

The idea that an entire choir of people would sing a song for her made her heart swell with bittersweet pain. To have spent so many years believing no one cared for her and that she was, indeed, not worth caring about now seemed so foolish. God loved her, and she was coming to believe that God's people cared about her too. It was almost too much to absorb, but she was happy to try to do so a little at a time.

"Fanny's songwriting career blossomed during her marriage, but her husband realized she was already fairly well known as Fanny Crosby, so he insisted she keep her name rather than take his." Eva smiled. "I always thought that was such a thoughtful and selfless thing for him to do."

"He m-m-must have loved her v-v-very m-m-much."

"From all accounts, he truly did. He even gave her the freedom to travel when she needed to in order to make a public appearance, which happened quite often, especially after she met the well-known composer William Bradbury. He had heard of her poetry and how her lyrics were often put to music. He thought they would be a perfect match, and it seems he was right, as they ended up writing many songs together." *Abuela* leaned back in her seat and looked up into the sky. "The words to the first hymn they wrote together are so simple and yet so meaningful. 'We are going, we are going, to a home beyond the skies, where the fields are robed in beauty, and the sunlight never dies.'" Eva turned her gaze toward Jolissa. "Sometimes I so long to be there."

"No!" Jolissa spoke before thinking, reacting only to the pain her *abuela*'s words had caused to her heart. "I d-d-don't want you to l-l-leave me!"

Eva's smile faded, and her eyes clouded over. "Oh, *mija*, I didn't mean it that way. I don't want to leave you either, especially since we've just begun to know each other." She leaned forward. "But you do realize I am a *viejita*, right? Just a little old woman without many years left."

Jolissa brushed the tears that had popped into her eyes. "I know, b-b-but I w-w-would m-m-miss you s-s-so much."

"Of course you would, *mija*. But now that you have become a child of God, we know that we will see each other again. When we die, it won't be the end. We will be together again with the Lord one day—forever."

The image of her parents' faces flashed into her mind, and she gasped. "M-m-my p-p-p-arents! I will s-s-s-see them again t-t-t-too, w-w-won't I?"

Eva smiled and nodded. "You most certainly will. And what a glorious reunion that will be!"

The flicker of hope that had barely kept burning for the last fourteen years now burst into full flame. She would see her parents again! This wasn't the end. They would be together for all eternity because they were all true believers.

A bubble of joy rolled up from deep within Jolissa and came out as laughter, surprising them both. She couldn't stop. Within moments, her *abuela* had joined her. Even Mario stretched and jumped up onto Jolissa's lap, purring as if he too wanted to be part of the celebration.

❇ ❇ ❇

JOLISSA MANAGED TO GET *Tío*'s dinner fixed and even sat and ate with him before heading back to church that evening. The man had remained sullen throughout the meal and didn't even comment when she slipped out the front door, Bible in hand. Joseph's moods and attitudes still unnerved Jolissa, but not to the point of nearly paralyzing her as they had before.

I haven't even been tempted to run out to my little hideaway in the alley.

The realization brought a smile to her lips as she walked toward Eva's house, enjoying the evening breeze because she'd remembered to wear a sweater this time.

Despite her newfound joy at knowing she was a beloved child of God, her heart began to race as she neared the spot where she'd seen the police take the man away, the house where the little girl with the sad eyes lived. Her steps slowed when the place came into view, and as she stopped beside the tree where she'd stood watching the drama unfold, she found herself breathing a silent prayer for the child's protection.

"It's very sad what happened there."

The voice startled her, and she pivoted to find a heavyset young woman carrying a toddler on her hip. Two slightly older children hovered nearby, one with his arms wrapped around the woman's legs.

"I'm s-s-s-sorry. Wh-wh-what did you s-s-say?"

"I said it's sad what happened there."

Jolissa nodded, realizing the woman must be referring to the man being arrested.

"W-w-was that the l-l-little girl's f-f-father?"

The woman sighed. "Yes. And it looks like he won't be coming home any time soon." She shook her head. "Not that I'm surprised. He was always drunk and getting into fights. I guess the last one caused some permanent damage."

Jolissa felt her eyes widen. What did that mean? She was about to ask when the woman went on.

"And then the *abuela* had a heart attack. I haven't heard how she is, have you?"

Eyes still wide, Jolissa shook her head no.

"Now Lupita is gone too." She shrugged. "Maybe it's for the best. Maybe she'll end up in a good foster home somewhere. Couldn't be much worse than it was here."

Lupita. So that was the little girl's name. But gone? Into foster care? *Tío* always told Jolissa that's what he had saved her from, so she had imagined it to be worse than life with her uncle. Yet this woman thought it might be better than living with a drunken father and an ailing grandmother. It was almost too much to comprehend.

The toddler began to fuss, and the woman excused herself, the older children following close behind as she continued down the street. But Jolissa didn't move. She returned her gaze to the now empty house and wondered what had happened to the child who once lived there.

Lupita. Why didn't I try to help her? Why didn't I do something?

The thought came to her then that it was not too late. She could pray for the little girl—for Lupita—and God would watch over her. With that assurance in her heart, she continued toward her *abuela*'s house.

✸ ✸ ✸

"OH, *MIJA*, I AM SO SORRY TO HEAR THIS," Eva said when Jolissa had finished recounting the event. "But you must not beat yourself up over it. There truly was nothing you could have done. Praying for her is the best thing. And now you have a name to pray for—Lupita."

Jolissa nodded. "And I w-w-will. Every d-d-day."

Abuela patted her hand as they stood in the entryway, ready to leave for church. "I know you will. God has put that little girl on your heart for a reason. You may not ever see her again in this lifetime, but you can be sure that your Father is listening to your prayers for her."

Eva picked up her Bible from the table by the door. With a light shawl around her shoulders, they stepped out onto the porch and headed for the sidewalk.

"It is a beautiful evening," *Abuela* commented. "But have you noticed that it's getting dark a little earlier now? It won't be long until winter is here." She chuckled. "Listen to me. Winter in Southern California! People who live back east would laugh if they heard me."

Jolissa forced a smile, still working at blocking out the memory of Lupita's sad eyes.

In minutes they had arrived at the church, and Jolissa heard the lively music spilling out the open doors onto the streets, inviting all to come. Oh, how she prayed that many would listen and respond so they too could find the joy and peace that she now knew as her own!

As they slipped into an empty pew, Eva laid her hand on Jolissa's arm. "*Mija*, do you have time to come home with me for a little while after church? I have something I would like to discuss with you."

Jolissa raised her eyebrows. Curious, she nodded. *Tio* would be fine until she got home, but she couldn't imagine what it was that her *abuela* had on her mind.

Chapter 18

THE SERVICE WAS COMING TO A CLOSE, and the pastor asked them to stand. "I understand we have a special request tonight, one of my favorite songs, 'Safe in the Arms of Jesus.' As we sing it, may it be our benediction. Rest safely in His arms, beloved."

The music began then, and Jolissa turned toward Eva, who smiled in return. "Th-th-thank y-y-y-you," Jolissa whispered. *Abuela* nodded, and then turned toward the front and began to sing. Jolissa followed along, reading the words on the screen.

> *Safe in the arms of Jesus, safe on His gentle breast,*
> *There by His love o'ershaded, sweetly my soul shall rest.*

Tears flooded her eyes as she thought of Lupita. *Safe in Your arms, Lord! Oh please, keep her safe!*

> *Jesus, my heart's dear Refuge, Jesus has died for me;*
> *Firm on the Rock of Ages, ever my trust shall be.*
> *Here let me wait with patience, wait till the night is over;*
> *Wait till I see the morning break on the golden shore.*

"Rock of Ages." They had sung that song just that morning. Jolissa's heart swelled with joy to think that she had found the safety of being held in Jesus' arms, of belonging to the Rock of Ages. As the congregation sang, she prayed that the little girl called Lupita would find that same place of safety and refuge.

✳ ✳ ✳

THERE WAS A SLIGHT CHILL in the air by the time Jolissa and Eva walked home, so they opted for hot tea as they sat at the kitchen table, discussing the evening service.

"I s-s-still c-c-can't believe they s-s-sang that song I w-w-wanted to h-h-hear. H-h-how did y-y-you g-g-get them t-t-to do it so s-s-soon?"

Abuela set her cup down and smiled. "I didn't. I just made a phone call and a suggestion, but the choir director thought it would be perfect for tonight's closing song. See how God works things out, even down to the little details of our lives?"

Jolissa was still getting used to the idea that God cared about her at all, let alone something as minute as her wanting to hear a particular song. But she sure was glad He did.

"You s-s-said y-y-you w-w-wanted to t-t-t-talk to me about s-s-something?"

Eva nodded, pausing as Jolissa wondered again what it might be. She sure hoped it wasn't anything bad. Had she been making a nuisance of herself, coming over too often?

"I have a couple of things I want to show you." Eva got up and walked to the key rack hanging by the back door. She lifted a key off its hook and returned to the table.

"This is the key to my car." She set it between them. "It's an old Honda Civic, a 2003, but as far as I know it's in good condition." She shrugged. "It has less than 10,000 miles on it because I've hardly driven it since I bought it new.

I haven't driven it at all in the last three years. My eyesight, you know."

Jolissa wasn't surprised that her nearly eighty-three-year-old *abuela*'s eyes were failing, but she was truly surprised to learn that she had a car.

"Wh-where is it? I've n-n-never seen it."

Eva chuckled. "That's because I don't drive it anymore and you've never been in my garage. Would you like to see it now?"

Jolissa nodded. "S-s-sure."

Eva led her out into the backyard, through the patio, and on to the small detached garage. A weed-infested driveway spilled out from its double doors, leading past the side of the house toward the street. Jolissa wondered why she'd never noticed it before.

She helped her *abuela* tug the doors open and waited as Eva turned on the lights. In the midst of boxes and old pieces of furniture and several suitcases sat a small, tan sedan, covered in several layers of dust.

"As you can see, not only haven't I driven it, but I haven't washed it either. Didn't seem to be much point."

It was hard enough to picture her *abuela* driving a car, but she could never imagine her washing one. Then again, Jolissa realized, there were probably a lot of things the now elderly woman used to do before they met—when she was still young and with a very different life than she presently had.

"Would you like to take it for a ride sometime?"

Jolissa jerked her head toward Eva. "Wh-wh-what?"

Abuela smiled and held out the key. "I think there's gas in it. We could try it tonight if you'd like. My neighbor starts it for me every now and then to make sure the battery is still good, so it should run. What do you think?"

What did she think? About driving *Abuela*'s car? Now?

"I . . . I d-d-don't know."

Eva's outstretched hand still held the key, but Jolissa couldn't force herself to take it. Sure, she'd taken driving lessons and even had her license, but she hadn't driven in a very long time. She and *Tío* didn't have a car, so driving had faded from her realm of possibilities.

Until now. Was *Abuela* serious? It certainly seemed so.

"Would you be more comfortable waiting until tomorrow? After work, maybe? I know you said you needed to get home soon, but maybe we could take it out for a ride tomorrow afternoon?" She smiled, and her eyes twinkled. "We might even consider taking it through a car wash."

Jolissa swallowed. A myriad of reasons not to do it ran through her mind, but she dismissed them all. Instead she nodded. "T-t-tomorrow would be g-g-great. I'll c-c-come right after w-w-w-work."

Eva dropped the key into her pocket and clapped her hands. "Wonderful! It's a date. I'm so excited, aren't you?"

Jolissa wasn't sure if she was excited or terrified, but apparently she'd just made a date, and she knew she would keep it.

* * *

EVA POPPED INTO THE CHURCH on Monday morning to straighten up the sanctuary after the previous evening's services. It was almost the reverse of what she did on Fridays to prepare for the weekend, and it was a simple job— picking up some discarded bulletins and a tissue or two— but she enjoyed it. Volunteering at the church helped give her life meaning when she often felt there was little else she could contribute.

And then You brought Jolissa into my life. She smiled as she retrieved a crumpled bulletin. *I can't thank You enough,*

Father. It is such an honor to be part of Your plan to bring someone to Yourself.

She thought then of Jolissa's face when Eva offered to let her drive the car. Excitement danced in her own stomach as she considered their planned outing that afternoon. She knew Jolissa wouldn't be available for several hours, but Eva wanted to get home in time to make something special for lunch before they went out for their ride. *Albondigas?* She smiled. She loved the flavorful soup with the tiny meatballs. Would Jolissa like it?

One way to find out. Scanning the final row and finding it devoid of any trash, she made her way toward the door leading to the office, already thinking about how much fun it would be to one day teach Jolissa to make *albondigas*. But for now, Eva would let the secretary know she was leaving before heading back out into the warm morning sunshine.

"Ah, are you done so soon?"

The middle-aged woman named Felicity sat at her desk, smiling up at her. At least, Eva assumed there was a desk under all that paperwork. But she'd never seen Felicity's desk looking any other way, so she imagined this was normal.

"Yes. I'm having company for lunch today, and I think I'll fix some *albondigas*."

Felicity's eyes widened. "Oh, Mrs. Pedrosa, I remember when you brought a big pot of that to the church supper. It was wonderful!" She glanced at her messy desk and then sighed before looking back up at Eva. "If I wasn't so far behind, I'd invite myself to join you."

Eva laughed. "And I would say you are most welcome. Maybe we can do it another time."

"That would be great. So is it anyone I know? Your lunch date, I mean. A grandchild, maybe?"

Eva smiled and nodded. "Yes. My granddaughter is coming for lunch. And then she's going to take me for a drive in my car."

"Sounds like a perfect day."

Eva agreed and turned to leave, but stopped when the side door leading to the playground burst open. A frazzled-looking child-care worker stepped inside, two preschoolers in tow.

"Any progress on finding another child-care assistant? We're running as fast as we can out there, but we seriously need more help."

Eva noticed that one of the children sucked her thumb, while the other one had a runny nose and needed a tissue. She pulled one from her pocket and bent down.

"There you go," she said, wiping away the problem. She smiled at the harried young woman, whose name tag read *Miss Janet*.

"If I were twenty years younger, I might apply for the job myself."

Miss Janet nodded. "And we would hire you in a heartbeat. If you know anyone, send them our way, will you? It needs to be someone who can pass a background check, of course, and preferably someone with a degree or currently studying in a field related to early childhood development or social work."

The child who had been sucking her thumb pulled it out of her mouth and began pulling Miss Janet's hands, whining about going outside to play.

"We're desperate!" She turned her attention to Felicity. "So . . . nothing yet?"

"Afraid not. We're looking, though."

With a sigh, Miss Janet allowed her tiny charges to lead her back to the playground. Eva reminded herself that she had been about to leave and turned toward the other door to do so, even as another new idea began forming in her mind.

Chapter 19

IT WAS ESPECIALLY HOT IN THE BACK ROOM that morning, and Jolissa was pouring sweat as she counted down the last fifteen minutes before she got off. She had mixed emotions about going to her *abuela*'s today, knowing she was supposed to take the car out for a drive. She had taken driver training when she was a senior in high school and had gotten her license, but she hadn't driven since. Would she even remember how?

"Jolissa?"

She looked up, surprised to find Mr. Peterson standing in front of her. Sweat beaded on his forehead and upper lip. *So he's feeling the heat too.* Still holding the shirt she'd been pressing, she offered a hesitant smile.

"Y-yes?"

He shifted from one foot to the other and then took a deep breath before beginning, "I, uh . . . I know I said I was going to give you and Marianne part-time work so I could keep you both, but . . . well, it's just not working out. As you know, Marianne has kids, and . . . well, the bottom line is, she needs more hours. More money. And she needs it more than you do. Do you understand what I'm saying?"

A faint ringing began in Jolissa's ears, but she tried to shake it off. Surely Mr. Peterson wasn't firing her, was he? "I d-d-don't understand."

Mr. Peterson nodded. "I know. And I wish I didn't have to do this, but . . . I just can't give Marianne more hours and keep you on too." He shrugged. "I'm sorry, Jolissa. You're a good worker, but . . . I'm just going to have to let you go. You can finish out this week, but Friday will be your last day."

The buzzing increased, and Jolissa tried to speak but her mouth had gone dry. Friday? Her last day? No more job? It was bad enough cutting back to part-time, but now this. What would she do? What would she tell her *tio*?

Mr. Peterson cleared his throat. "Well, like I said, I'm really sorry."

When she still didn't respond, he turned and walked away. Jolissa watched him disappear through the door to the office, but still she didn't move. What was she supposed to do now? She had no answer but to finish her shift and then clock out and go to *Abuela*'s house. Surely the wise old woman would have some advice. And even if she didn't, she would surely pray for Jolissa. Right now that was what she wanted more than anything.

* * *

"I j-j-just d-d-don't understand, *Abuela*. Wh-wh-why w-w-would God l-l-let me l-l-lose m-m-my job? He knows I n-n-need it."

They sat across from one another at the kitchen table, with half-eaten bowls of *albondigas* cooling in front of them. Jolissa really enjoyed the soup, and she appreciated her *abuela*'s efforts to make it. But as hard as she tried to take her mind off losing her job, she simply couldn't stop thinking about it.

For probably the fourth or fifth time since Jolissa arrived, Eva tried to comfort her. "God knows what He's doing, *mija*. When one door closes, another one opens, as they say—whoever 'they' are. But seriously, maybe it's time for a better job. After all, you said you were having trouble getting by on part-time pay."

Jolissa nodded. "I . . . I know. That's t-t-true. But . . ." She forced a smile. "I n-n-need to l-l-let it g-g-go, don't I? And I'm t-t-trying."

"I know you are, *mija*. And I know it's not easy. But we've prayed, and God is going to lead you to the answer He has for you. You need to be patient and trust Him. Can you do that?"

Swallowing what felt like a giant rock in her throat, Jolissa nodded again. "I'll try."

"And I'll help you." Eva smiled. "Come on, now, finish your soup. We're going to take the car out for a ride, remember? We'll get it washed and . . . and then maybe stop by the church for a few minutes. Would that be all right?"

Jolissa raised her eyebrows and shrugged. "S-s-sure. Whatever y-y-you want to d-d-do, *Abuela*."

Eva nodded. "Good. Now, can I warm up your soup for you?"

Jolissa looked down at her bowl. She had to admit that it was the best *albondigas* she'd ever had, but then again she hadn't had it more than a couple of times in her life. She was pleased that *Abuela* had offered to teach her how to make it one of these days.

"Y-y-yes, please. It really is g-g-g-good. B-b-but you sit s-s-still. I'll g-g-get it. I'll r-r-refill y-y-y-yours too."

Abuela looked pleased as Jolissa picked up both bowls and carried them to the stove.

Jolissa's shoulders ached from gripping the steering wheel all the way to the car wash, but after sitting on the bench with *Abuela* for fifteen minutes, waiting for their sparkling clean coach to emerge from the soap-and-water tunnel, she had relaxed a bit. Maybe by the time they got to the church she'd feel at home behind the wheel again.

"There it is!" Eva stood up and pointed at the shiny vehicle being hand-dried by two workers with towels and chamois. "I'd forgotten how nice it looks when it's clean."

Jolissa stood up too, pleased at the results. "Y-y-you're r-r-right, *Abuela*. It l-l-looks g-g-great."

Within moments they were back in the front seat, driving the few blocks to the church parking lot. How different the otherwise familiar neighborhood seemed when viewed from the front seat of a car rather than on foot!

Jolissa smiled as they stepped out of the car. This driving thing really was beginning to feel a little less intimidating. Now to see why *Abuela* wanted to stop at church.

"Do y-y-you n-n-need some h-h-h-help with s-s-something?"

Eva raised her eyebrows, and Jolissa had the sense that her nonchalant look was forced. *Strange. I've never noticed that about her before.*

"Not really." *Abuela* smiled. "But I would like you to meet the secretary, Felicity. She's a very nice woman."

"I'd l-l-like th-th-that." Taking *Abuela*'s arm, Jolissa walked her around to the office entrance and then held the door while the older woman stepped inside.

"Ah, Mrs. Pedrosa, so nice to see you again. This must be the granddaughter you were telling me about."

Jolissa closed the door behind her and glanced at *Abuela*, who smiled reassuringly.

"It certainly is. Her name is Jolissa Montoya. Jolissa, this is Felicity Adams, our church secretary."

Felicity reached her hand up, and Jolissa shook it in greeting. "N-n-nice to m-m-meet y-y-you."

"Nice to meet you too." Felicity's eyebrows drew together, and she appeared to study Jolissa. "Haven't I seen you at church a time or two? With your grandmother?"

Jolissa nodded. "Y-y-yes. I've been c-c-coming l-l-lately."

"Wonderful! Well, we're so glad you've joined us." She turned her attention to Eva. "Is there something I can do for you today, or did you just come by to introduce your granddaughter?"

"Actually, I wondered if you were still looking for someone to work in the day care. Jolissa is studying to be a social worker and—"

Felicity's dark eyes widened, and she sucked in a breath, interrupting Eva midsentence. "Really?" She turned her gaze toward Jolissa. "Are you looking for a job?"

For the second time that day Jolissa heard a buzzing start up in her ears. What was going on? What was *Abuela* up to?

Jolissa realized both women were staring at her, waiting for an answer. She swallowed and tried to pull the words from her brain and push them out her mouth.

"I . . . I h-h-have a j-j-job. W-w-well, only until F-F-Friday. Then—"

Felicity shot out of her chair, and Jolissa took a step back. "So you're looking for a new job? In child care?"

"I . . . d-d-don't know. I g-g-guess s-s-so, b-b-but I d-d-don't know if I qu-qu-qualify."

Felicity waved her away. "That's for our director, Mrs. Feingold, to decide. Let me get her. I know she'll want to talk to you right away. Please, have a seat, both of you. I'll be right back."

Too stunned to argue, she followed *Abuela*'s lead and sat down in one of the chairs by the wall. She turned to ask her *abuela* what was going on, but the old woman stared straight ahead, smiling. Without looking, she reached her wrinkled hand across to Jolissa's and patted it. And once again, Jolissa realized there was more to her newly adopted *abuela* than she'd realized.

Chapter 20

"I s-s-still c-c-can't believe I g-g-got that j-j-j-job, and th-th-that I'm s-s-starting on M-M-Monday."

The two women sat in Eva's backyard now, enjoying a cold drink before Jolissa had to head home to fix her *tio*'s dinner. Mario dozed on her lap, and Jolissa thought that even *Tio*'s worst mood couldn't ruin her day now.

"God is amazing, isn't He, *mija*? And His timing is always perfect."

"Do y-y-you th-th-think He d-d-did this f-f-for me?" The thought had been stirring around inside her since they left the church, but it was still a stretch for her to think that God Himself cared about such details.

Abuela smiled, her eyes closed as she tipped her face toward the sun. "I cannot say for certain, *mija*, for God's ways are far beyond our understanding. But I can tell you that the Bible says every good and perfect gift comes from our heavenly Father, and this is certainly a good gift, wouldn't you say?"

Jolissa smiled. "*Sí*. One of th-th-the b-b-best I ever g-g-got."

Abuela nodded. "Well, then, there's your answer."

Jolissa chewed her lip. "I'm a l-l-l-little n-n-n-nervous, though. Do y-y-you th-th-think I c-c-can handle it?"

Eva opened her eyes and turned to face Jolissa. "Oh, *mija*, this job was made for you. You have a heart for little ones, and now you'll have a chance to help care for them while you finish your schooling." Her smile was warm as she reached over and laid her hand on Jolissa's arm. "Just remember to pray each day and ask God to make you a blessing to those children."

Jolissa nodded. "I w-w-will." She hesitated but decided she had to ask. "But wh-wh-what about the w-w-way I t-t-talk? Wh-wh-what if the k-k-kids can't understand m-m-me?"

Eva patted her arm. "You let God take care of that, *mija*. The Bible says God wove you together in your mother's womb. That means He knows everything about you . . . and He doesn't make mistakes. So just relax and trust Him. And besides, remember what the director told you about your Spanish. Even though you're not fluent, you'll be a big help with those children whose first language is also Spanish."

Jolissa nodded again, then glanced at her watch. "I n-n-need to g-g-get going. *T-T-Tio* will be l-l-looking for m-m-m-me."

They rose from their chairs and started for the kitchen. Mario, disturbed from his nap, followed close behind, meowing in complaint.

"You know," Eva said as Jolissa held the door open for her, "you did very well driving my car today."

Jolissa raised her eyebrows. "Do y-y-you really th-th-think s-s-so?"

"I know so. And it did my heart good to know that my car was being used for its purpose once again."

Inside now, Jolissa retrieved her backpack from the kitchen table and bent down to say good-bye to Mario.

"In fact, I was thinking that maybe you should drive it more often."

Jolissa rose up and looked into her *abuela*'s face. "R-r-really? Well, y-y-you know I'd b-b-be glad to t-t-take you anywhere y-y-you w-w-want to g-g-go."

"That would be very nice, *mija*." Eva smiled. "But that's not exactly what I meant."

Jolissa frowned. "I d-d-don't understand."

"I've been thinking that you need that car much more than I do. Here it just sits in the garage all the time, gathering dust. But if you had it, you could drive it to school, to work, to church . . . and over here to see me, of course."

Jolissa's eyes widened, and she felt her knees go weak. Was her *abuela* offering to let her use the car?

"It would be a simple thing for us to go to the DMV and sign the car over to you as a gift. What do you think, *mija*?"

Jolissa pulled out one of the kitchen chairs and sank down in it. A gift? *Abuela* wanted to *give* the car to her?

She shook her head. "I d-d-don't know wh-wh-wh-what to s-s-say. I—"

Eva sat down next to her and took her hand, the faint and now familiar fragrance of lilacs teasing Jolissa's nostrils. "You don't have to say anything now. Just go home and think and pray about it. We can talk about it another time. Until you decide, you can just drive it when we're together and need to go somewhere. Even though I don't drive it myself, I always keep it fully insured and with up-to-date tags, just in case."

The warmth of her *abuela*'s hand sent a surge of courage to her heart, but her mind still reeled. She would most definitely have to think and pray about such an important decision. And then there was *Tio* to consider . . .

✳ ✳ ✳

Jolissa had weathered her uncle's mood swings and made it through two more days of work at the cleaners. She told Mr. Peterson and Marianne about her new job beginning the following week, and both seemed genuinely pleased. Even the butterflies in her stomach had settled down a bit, though she still found herself doubting her ability to take on the responsibility of child-care assistant.

Deep down, however, she was thrilled, and the upcoming job change had even birthed a new excitement and confidence in her studies. Best of all, it was Wednesday evening, and she was once again skipping class to attend church with *Abuela*. She knew she wouldn't be able to continue doing so each week, but she'd put in for a class transfer at school so she could get Wednesday evenings off. Having learned from *Abuela*, she prayed for favor that the transfer would be approved.

Now she stood on Eva's front porch, waiting for the door to open. When it did, she welcomed the hug she received.

"Come in, *mija*. Mario and I have been waiting for you."

The cat appeared as Jolissa stepped inside, and he immediately began purring and rubbing up against her leg. She knelt down to pet him, snuggling his soft fur.

"I have the keys and my Bible and my jacket," Eva announced. "I'm ready to go when you are."

Jolissa stood to her feet, her eyes focusing on the car keys in her *abuela*'s outstretched hand.

"Y-you w-w-want me t-t-to d-d-drive again?"

Abuela laughed. "Of course I do, *mija*. We didn't get that old car washed just so it could sit in the garage and get dirty all over again." She laid the keys in Jolissa's hand. "Have you prayed about accepting my gift?"

Jolissa swallowed. She had, and everything in her cried out to take it. And yet—

"It's t-t-too m-m-much. I c-c-can't accept—"

"Of course you can, *mija*. I wouldn't offer it if I didn't really want you to take it."

"B-b-but your f-f-family. Maybe th-th-they w-w-want it, or—"

Eva waved away the thought. "They already have cars; you don't. They don't need another one; you do. It's just that simple." She smiled. "Besides, *mija*, you are my family too, you know."

Jolissa's heart clenched. She knew the old woman spoke the truth. They had indeed become family. But was that reason enough to accept the car? And besides, she hadn't even mentioned it to *Tío* yet. What would he think of such a thing?

"Come," Eva said, gently tugging Jolissa's arm. "We can discuss this later. First we must go to church. Mario will take care of things while we're gone. Right, Mario?"

The cat meowed, and the two women headed out the back door to the garage, Jolissa's heart and mind still wrestling with her decision.

* * *

"I THOUGHT IT WAS INTERESTING that Pastor quoted Isaiah 42:16, didn't you?"

Jolissa steered the car down the darkened streets toward Eva's home. She'd loved the service and had taken note of several verses to look up in her Bible and study more when she got home, but offhand she couldn't remember what the one from Isaiah said.

"Wh-wh-which one, *Abuela*?"

Eva quoted it from memory: "I will bring the blind by a way they did not know; I will lead them in paths they have not known. I will make darkness light before them, and crooked places straight. These things I will do for them, and not forsake them." The old woman sighed. "I've always loved the verse, but it is especially meaningful when you think of Fanny Crosby's amazing life, don't you think?"

Jolissa nodded, though she knew her *abuela* couldn't see her. "Y-y-yes. I th-th-thought of her wh-wh-when the p-p-p-astor r-r-read it."

"I know you can't stay for more of the story this evening, but let me tell you just a little bit while we drive. Do you mind?"

"I w-w-w-would l-l-love it."

"Fanny wrote many hymns during her lifetime, some under pen names, and quite a few won awards. But the first one that really gained her worldwide notice was called 'Pass Me Not, O Gentle Savior.' I love the story behind it.

"It was in 1868, after she spoke about Jesus at a prison service. One of the prisoners cried out, 'O Lord, don't pass me by!' She later wrote the famous hymn from that prisoner's brief, heartfelt cry. In a short time, the song was being sung all over the world. One night, during revival meetings in London, an Englishman who was known for his hard drinking and living heard the song and whispered to himself, 'Oh, I wish He would not pass me by.' Before the revival services ended, the man was saved. Then he began carrying a copy of the hymn with him everywhere he went, and when he eventually moved to America and became a successful businessman, he had the opportunity to meet Fanny and to give her twenty dollars—which of course was a much larger sum then than it is now."

Jolissa considered the story as she pulled into Eva's driveway. "F-F-Fanny n-n-never knew all th-th-the p-p-people she h-h-helped, did sh-sh-she?"

"None of us does, *mija*." She laid her hand on Jolissa's. "And just as he led Fanny in her darkness, God will do the same for you."

Chapter 21

JOLISSA SAID GOOD-BYE TO HER BOSS and co-worker on Friday afternoon and left for home. She even bypassed Eva's house because she had decided to talk to *Tio* about her *abuela*'s offer of a car and also the job change. She had no idea how he would take either piece of news, but the confrontation wasn't going to get any easier by putting it off.

She scarcely noticed the unusually cool breeze that tossed her hair as she walked. All she could do was pray that God would help her explain these things to *Tio* and that he would react calmly and rationally.

That would be a miracle, Lord. You know better than I do that Tio *is not a calm or rational man. Please help me not to be afraid.*

She let herself in the front door, not surprised to find her uncle in his usual spot in front of the TV.

"Hello, *T-T-Tio*," she called as she crossed the room to stand beside his wheelchair. Her heart thumped against her ribcage as he raised his face to hers, a scowl already darkening his features.

"So you decided to come straight home for a change." His growl dripped with sarcasm. "What's the matter? Were your so-called friends too busy for you?" He smirked before turning back to his program.

"I . . . c-c-came home to t-t-tell you s-s-some news, *T-T-Tio*."

He shook his head. "I'm busy now. Can't you see that? I don't have time to listen to your stuttering. You can tell me your news at dinner."

Jolissa thought of reminding him that she had school that evening and wouldn't be able to linger over dinner with him, but she thought better of it. Maybe spitting it out all at once, short and sweet, after placing his meal on the table was the best strategy. If he became unbearable, she could grab her things and leave for school a little early.

She surveyed the refrigerator. There was enough leftover chicken to make some soup, and *Tio* always seemed to like that—at least, as much as he liked anything. She grabbed an onion, some celery and a few carrots, and then began chopping.

The table was set and she was about to ladle the soup into bowls when her uncle rolled his wheelchair in behind her. "So, what's your big news?" Once again sarcasm laced his words. "I can hardly wait to hear it."

She set the ladle down and turned to him. It was now or never.

"I . . . I g-g-got a n-n-n-new j-j-job. At th-th-the ch-ch-church, w-w-working with k-k-kids. I s-s-start on M-M-M-Monday."

Joseph stared at her, his eyes wide, as she waited. When his laugh exploded from him at last, it nearly knocked Jolissa off her feet.

"You? Working at the church?" He laughed some more. "And with kids? How are you going to do that? They won't even understand you when you talk." He shook his head, and the laughter shut down. "You are an *idiota*. I always knew it. Do you really think anyone else will be as patient with you as I am? Who else would put up with your stuttering and stammering all day long?" He shook his head again. "No, it will never work. At least at the cleaners you don't have to speak to anyone. That is a better job for you. You must stay there."

Jolissa felt the sweat popping on her forehead, but she stood her ground. "I c-c-can't, *Tio*. I g-g-got l-l-laid off. Mr. P-P-Peterson said th-th-there's n-n-not enough w-w-work."

Any sign of laughter had long since disappeared from *Tio*'s face. His scowl was back, darker than ever. "You got fired?" His voice rose to a roar. "Fired? Who gets fired from a simple job at the cleaners? An *idiota*, that's who! And now what? You think you can work at a church? Ha! As soon as you talk to them they will fire you, and then what will we do? Do you think I can pay all the bills with my disability check? How are we supposed to manage? What an ungrateful girl you are! Stupid and ungrateful. After all I've done for you, this is how you thank me."

He wheeled around and pushed himself from the kitchen, leaving Jolissa trembling in front of the stove. What should she do? *Help me, Lord. Show me.*

Responding to the only thought that popped into her head, she spooned out *Tio*'s soup, set it on the table, and then snagged her backpack and headed out the door. She was halfway to school before she realized she hadn't even mentioned the car.

* * *

SCHOOL WENT SMOOTHLY, but when it was over Jolissa still wasn't ready to return home. Since she hadn't stopped by to see her *abuela* after work that afternoon, she decided to do so now—but only if her kitchen light was still on. *Abuela* had mentioned to her more than once that she turned it off when she went to bed.

A wave of relief passed over her when she turned the corner and saw the kitchen light still burning. She promised herself she wouldn't stay long, but she really needed some wise counsel and a little comfort too.

"*Mija*!" Eva's face lit up the moment she opened the door and saw Jolissa standing on the porch. "I'm so glad you came. I missed you today. Come in. Tell me about school—and your last day of work at the cleaners."

The women had no sooner made their way into the kitchen than Mario padded into the room and invited himself onto Jolissa's lap.

"I was just about to have a little snack before bedtime. You're just in time to join me."

Jolissa watched the old woman, who was already dressed in a flannel robe and wearing slippers, rummage in the refrigerator. "How about some of that flan we made? There's still quite a bit left."

Jolissa's cheeks heated up at the memory of her *abuela*'s offer to take some of the flan home and how she'd turned it down because of the memory of what her *tio* had done the last time she'd brought food home with her. But a growling stomach now reminded her that she'd left home before dinner, and she had to admit that the flan sounded delicious. Within moments they were seated together at the table, sharing the scrumptious dessert.

"So, *mija*, you said good-bye at work, yes?"

Jolissa nodded. "I d-d-did. And they w-w-were v-v-very kind." She smiled between bites. "They even g-g-gave me a l-l-little going-away p-p-party w-w-with c-c-cupcakes."

"How nice! I know you appreciated that."

"I d-d-did. And th-th-they w-w-wished me w-w-well at my n-n-new j-j-job."

"And your *tio*?" Abuela paused, setting her spoon down and squinting a bit as she studied Jolissa's face. "What did he say about your new job?"

The flan lost its creamy sweetness as Jolissa swallowed a mouthful and summoned the words to answer *Abuela*'s question. Taking a deep breath, she did her best to explain to Eva what had happened. When she finished, tears rimmed the old woman's eyes.

"I am so sorry, *mija*. I know that was very hard for you."

Jolissa nodded. "Now I . . . I d-d-don't know wh-wh-what to d-d-do. Should I s-s-say anything else t-t-to him about it, or j-j-just avoid the t-t-topic?"

Eva sighed. "I have no clear answer for you, but before you go home we will pray that God will show you." She took Jolissa's hand and squeezed it. "He will guide you, *mija*, even as He guided Fanny Crosby in her dark times."

Bits and pieces of the verse from Isaiah flitted through Jolissa's mind, and she reminded herself to read it again when she got home.

"I'll be right back." Eva rose from the table and returned moments later with the quilt. She sat back down and showed a square to Jolissa.

"We started talking about some of the stories behind Fanny's songs, so I thought you should see this patch. It's a musical note, see? And what a huge part of Fanny's life it turned out to represent!"

Jolissa smiled. She somehow sensed that what her *abuela* was about to tell her was just what she needed to hear.

"I told you about how it's believed that 'Safe in the Arms of Jesus' was written in response to the loss of Fanny and Alexander's baby daughter, didn't I?"

Jolissa nodded, her heart squeezing at the thought of the pain the couple must have endured.

"I don't think any of her other songs produced so many wonderful testimonials as that one. I'll tell you just a few of the stories that came to light as a result of it."

She laid the quilt in her lap and appeared to be gathering her thoughts. "The first one that comes to my mind is about a bishop by the last name of Hannington. He was serving in Uganda when he was murdered by those he had gone to try and help. His diary was found sometime later, and in it he told of how he was singing that wonderful song even up until the moment they came and dragged him away, leaving the diary behind."

The very thought of such courage in the face of a horrible death caused Jolissa's cheeks to burn with the shame of how she cowered before her uncle's harsh words. What she suffered seemed so minor in comparison.

"One of my favorite stories that came out of the writing of that song was about a hackman—the equivalent of a taxi driver in those days—who discovered his passenger was Fanny Crosby. He was taking Fanny to catch a train, but when he realized who she was, he stopped the vehicle, took off his hat, and burst into tears. Then he called a policeman and asked him to please escort Fanny to the train, as he was too overwrought to do it himself." She leaned forward. "It seems his little girl had died just the week before and they sang 'Safe in the Arms of Jesus' at her funeral."

Tears sprang to Jolissa's eyes. So much sorrow in the world! And yet Fanny Crosby had found a way to use God's gifts to her to help others through their pain. Was it possible she would one day be able to do the same?

"And then there's the amazing story of the Finnish engineer, a former army officer named Nordenberg, who came to Christ in a most unusual way in 1918." She took a deep breath and continued. "It seems the army in Finland had taken several prisoners from the Red Army, their enemy. Seven of the captives were sentence to death. One of them had recently heard the song 'Safe in the Arms of Jesus' at a Salvation Army meeting. He began to sing it as he awaited his execution. As he sang, the other six prisoners fell to their knees and raised their arms to heaven. All seven of them sang the song with their dying breaths. It was that stunning testimony of faith that brought Nordenberg to Christ."

"All b-b-because of a s-s-song."

Eva's smile was sweet as she patted Jolissa's hand. "All because of the One who gave Fanny that song, the same One who has a great purpose for your life too, *mija*."

Abuela closed her eyes then and began to pray aloud for Jolissa and the situation with her *tio*, as well as about her new job. Jolissa closed her eyes and joined her in prayer.

✳ ✳ ✳

JOLISSA HAD BEEN RELIEVED when she came into the house Friday night and discovered that her uncle had already gone to bed. She went to her room and picked up her Bible, then read and reread Isaiah 42:16 before falling into a sound sleep.

Saturday morning was gray and overcast, which is perhaps why Jolissa slept in a bit later than usual. She could hear her uncle in the bathroom before she climbed out of bed. Racing to the kitchen, she got the coffee started. Breakfast was on the table by the time she heard him emerge from the bathroom.

Reminding herself of the stories of sorrow and courage she'd heard from her *abuela* the night before, she prayed as she waited for her *tio* to join her at the breakfast table. But he didn't.

After a few minutes she rose to her feet and peered from the kitchen doorway into the living room, and then into the hallway. He was nowhere in sight, but his bedroom door was closed. It had been open when she walked by earlier, while he was still in the bathroom. *Strange. He always comes straight from the bathroom to the kitchen, every morning.*

Puzzled, she approached his room. "*Tio?*" She waited. When no answer came, she tried again. "*T-T-Tio?* Are y-y-you all r-r-right?"

A moan floated through the door, and she quickly pushed it open. Her uncle lay on his bed, fully dressed, his hand on his chest.

"*Tio!*" She rushed to his side. "Wh-wh-what is it? Do y-y-you need a d-d-doctor? Should I c-c-call n-n-nine-one-one?"

"*Idiota!*" His voice was scarcely above a whisper as he waved her away. "I am fine. Just tired, that's all. Leave me alone."

"B-b-but, *Tio*—"

"Go!" His voice was slightly stronger now. "Leave me alone. Let me rest."

Her heart thrummed against her chest in protest, but she knew it was useless to argue with him. Slowly she turned and crept from the room, though she left the door open enough so she could check on him.

At least I don't have to go anywhere. I'll stay here all day and keep an eye on him—and pray.

She hurried to the kitchen and picked up the phone to call her *abuela*. It would be nice to know that she was praying as well.

Chapter 22

Jolissa had hesitated in leaving her *tio* alone while she went to church on Sunday, but he had insisted he was fine and practically ordered her out of the house. And she had to admit that he had seemed much better that morning, so she'd walked to *Abuela*'s, where they'd decided to walk the short distance to church rather than drive, and now they were climbing the steps of the Light House entrance.

Already the music drew her as she and Eva stepped inside and proceeded up the middle aisle. The service wouldn't begin for nearly fifteen minutes, but a few early worshippers drifted in along with them. As the two women settled into a pew toward the front, one middle-aged woman in particular seemed to be studying them. When their eyes met, Jolissa offered her a weak smile and then bent her head to read the bulletin.

"Excuse me."

Jolissa raised her head to find the woman standing at the end of the aisle where they sat. Eva had looked up at her too but didn't immediately greet her, so Jolissa wondered if they might not know one another. It seemed her *abuela* knew almost everyone at the church, but perhaps this person was an exception. Besides, she was focused on Jolissa, not Eva.

"Forgive me, but . . . you look so familiar. Actually, I should say that you remind me of someone I used to know . . .

before she and her husband were killed in a car accident. But she had a daughter who would be about your age now, and the resemblance is so strong. I just wondered if . . ."

Jolissa's heart hammered in her chest, and her mouth went dry. Was it possible this woman had known her parents? But how could she? Jolissa and her family had lived miles from here and knew no one in the immediate area, other than her *tio*.

Eva laid her hand on Jolissa's arm, as if to encourage her and help her respond.

"Wh-wh-what was y-y-your friend's n-n-name?"

The woman's brows drew together. "It was Marta Montoya. Her husband's name was Ricardo. They had one child, a little girl with an unusual name. I can't remember it after all these years, but as I said, she would have been about your age. And you truly do resemble Marta."

Tears bit Jolissa's eyes, and she tried to push past the lump in her throat. She nodded her head and forced herself to speak. "Y-y-yes. Th-th-that was my m-m-mother's name. I'm J-J-J-Jolissa M-M-Montoya."

The woman's eyebrows raised and her hand flew to her chest. "Oh, I can hardly believe it! Little Jolissa! Of course, I remember your name now." Her expression switched to stricken as she continued. "It was such a tragedy about your parents. They were absolutely wonderful neighbors. I felt so bad for you and always wondered what happened to you. I heard you went to live with a relative, but I had no idea where. And now I've run across you here! It's a miracle."

Jolissa thought the woman was probably right. She didn't really remember her, but over the years she'd wondered about people from her early childhood. Never had she imagined to see any of them again, though, and the realization nearly took her breath away.

"This is wonderful," *Abuela* said, drawing Jolissa's attention as she gently squeezed her arm. "Absolutely wonderful!"

The woman smiled at Eva and held out her hand. "Forgive me. I should have introduced myself. My name is Susan Woodward. I'm here visiting a friend for the weekend."

Eva shook the woman's hand. "And I'm Eva Pedrosa, Jolissa's adopted grandma."

Jolissa's heart warmed at her *abuela*'s identification with her, even as she found the woman's name hiding in her memory banks. Yes, she did remember her now. A nice woman who lived a couple doors away from them before—

She blinked her eyes and forced herself back to the present. Then she too shook Susan's hand. "I . . . I l-l-live w-w-with my *t-t-tio* now—m-m-my uncle."

Susan nodded, though she seemed a bit puzzled once again. "I see." She smiled. "Well, I would love to chat a bit, but my friend is waiting for me and the service is about to start. Maybe afterward?"

Jolissa and Eva exchanged glances in wordless agreement. "Th-th-that w-w-would be n-n-nice," Jolissa said.

"If you and your friend don't have plans after church, you're welcome to come to my home for lunch," Eva added. "It's only a few blocks from here."

Susan appeared genuinely disappointed. "Oh, I wish we could, but we actually do have somewhere we need to be this afternoon. But maybe we could at least catch up for a few minutes in the church courtyard."

They agreed, and Susan returned to her seat a few pews ahead of theirs. Jolissa watched her animated discussion with her friend, who peeked in Jolissa's direction a couple of times. Then the service started and she did her best to push the meeting from her mind.

EVA AND JOLISSA SAT at the kitchen table, eating soup and discussing the morning's service, as well as their surprise meeting with Susan and her friend, Joanne. Mario lay curled around Jolissa's feet.

Eva watched the young woman's reaction as she spoke to her. "Meeting Susan was quite an unexpected blessing for you, wasn't it, *mija?*"

Jolissa nodded, as a hint of wetness came and went from her eyes. "It's th-th-the first t-t-time I've s-s-seen anyone f-f-from . . . before."

"Before your parents died. Before you came to live with your *tio*."

Jolissa nodded again. Eva could feel her sadness. As she so often did, she covered Jolissa's hand with her own. "Do you want to talk about it?"

She hesitated, and then shrugged. "N-n-not right n-n-now, *Abuela*. D-d-do you m-m-m-mind?"

"Of course not. How about if I tell you another story about one of Fanny's songs?"

A smile spread across Jolissa's face. "Yes. Th-th-that w-w-would be n-n-nice."

"It happened in 1869, on a hot July night, when Fanny was speaking to a large group of men at a mission, men who had fallen on hard times for one reason or another. It was in a terrible section of New York known as the Bowery, but Fanny never hesitated to go anywhere she thought God had called her."

Eva saw a light flicker in Jolissa's eyes, but she said nothing.

"As Fanny spoke, she sensed that—in her words—some mother's son had to be rescued right away, that night, or he would be lost forever. She stopped in the middle of her delivery and gave an impassioned plea for salvation. Sure enough, a young man of about eighteen came forward. He told everyone there that he had promised to meet his mother in heaven but that he knew the way he was living it would never happen. Fanny then prayed with him to receive Jesus, and another soul was born into God's kingdom."

The tears that had teased Jolissa's eyes earlier flooded to the surface, and a couple of them spilled over. "Th-th-that's so b-b-beautiful."

Eva nodded. "Yes, it is. Can you imagine what it was like to be there? After Fanny prayed with him, he got up from his knees and told them that he now knew he would one day meet his mother in heaven because he had just met her God. Almost immediately after that Fanny began writing the words to 'Rescue the Perishing,' which has become one of her most popular hymns."

Jolissa brushed the tears from her eyes and shook her head. "I j-j-just w-w-wish I had h-h-half of F-F-Fanny's courage. B-b-but I c-c-c-can't even t-t-talk!"

Abuela breathed a silent prayer before speaking. "*Mija,* I want to tell you something that I learned from Susan Woodward while you were in the restroom. She confided in me that she was surprised to hear you stutter. She said you never did that as a child—not when she knew you anyway."

Jolissa's eyes widened, and she thought her heart would stop beating. She didn't stutter as a child before her parents died and she came to live with *Tio*? How was that possible and why didn't she remember it? Yet she somehow sensed that God had whispered a secret to her. If only she knew what she was supposed to do with it.

❋   ❋   ❋

STANDING AT THE STOVE, Jolissa fried a couple of pork chops for dinner. Mixed veggies simmered in a pot, and cole slaw waited in the fridge. As always, she would warm some tortillas to top it all off. *Tio* should be happy with dinner, but she was certain he'd find something to complain about.

She wasn't wrong.

"You fried the meat too long. You're twenty-one years old, and you still haven't learned how to cook. *Idiota!*"

He wrapped a piece of tortilla around another large chunk of chop slathered in salsa, and then stuffed it into his mouth. As he chewed a few drops of grease dribbled down his chin. Jolissa had learned it was better not to defend herself or respond in any way to his criticism. He wasn't going to back down anyway, so why bother? No sense provoking him further.

The meal felt like sawdust in her mouth, but she forced herself to clean her plate, chewing slowly and deliberately while *Tio* helped himself to seconds. It was obvious he had gotten over whatever had been ailing him the day before, so she had no qualms about leaving him alone again to return to church that evening.

After polishing off his second helping, *Tio* pushed himself away from the table. "Clean up this mess before you leave tonight," he growled, wheeling himself into the living room where the TV awaited him.

Don't I always? Jolissa longed to shout the question at him, but of course she didn't. Instead she asked God to forgive her for her sarcastic and defensive attitude. She silently finished her food and then stood to clear the table. *I didn't always stutter. I wasn't like this before my parents died and I came to live with* Tio.

The amazing revelation had been rolling around in her mind since she'd left *Abuela*'s that afternoon. She'd thought about it, asked God about it, even written it down in her journal and studied it in her own handwriting. But nothing had changed. *Tío* still hated her, and she still stuttered.

It's nice that You showed me this, Lord, she prayed silently as she placed the dishes in the sink full of soapy water. *But what good is it if I can't change anything?*

She pushed the thoughts from her mind and determined to finish the dishes so she could leave for *Abuela*'s house. She told herself she just had to accept that there were some things in life that never changed—and her stuttering was one of those things.

Chapter 23

Jolissa's palms were moist and her throat dry as she waited for the child-care director to escort her to the classroom where she would serve as teacher's assistant to fifteen three- and four-year-olds. What had she been thinking? Whatever made her imagine that she could handle such a job? She needed to be able to communicate with these little ones, and she couldn't figure out how she could possibly do that.

Maybe it's not too late to change my mind. Surely they'd understand if I told them I can't take the job after all. Besides, what were they thinking when they offered it to me in the first place? They must have been really desperate to give this job to someone like me.

Her *tio's* mocking words echoed in her ears, feeding the fire of fear that burned in her, urging her to escape before it was too late. But her feet felt nailed to the floor. As much as she wanted to run out the door before the director returned, she simply couldn't make herself move.

"So sorry to keep you waiting, Jolissa." Mrs. Feingold breezed into the room, looking impeccable in her navy blue slacks and crisply pressed white blouse. Felicity had confided in her that the director was in her midfifties, but Jolissa thought she didn't look a day over forty. If only she could be half as poised and self-assured! But then, Mrs. Feingold no doubt did not have a speech impediment.

The woman took her by the arm and gently nudged her toward the door that she herself had just entered. "Come, I'll walk you in. Miss Ginny is expecting you."

Miss Ginny. The teacher she had met briefly the previous week. Jolissa had to admit that she'd liked her right away. The woman was only about ten years older than Jolissa, and not quite as tall. She wore her long, blonde hair pulled back into a ponytail, which she explained made working with the children much easier. Jolissa had followed her advice and pulled her own hair back as well.

She and Mrs. Feingold had no sooner stepped into the classroom than fifteen sets of eyeballs turned in their direction. The children were sitting cross-legged on the floor, listening to Miss Ginny read a story.

"I told the children you were coming," Miss Ginny said, smiling as she set the book down and rose to her feet. "They're so excited to meet you." She turned toward the children. "Boys and girls, this is Miss Jolissa. She's going to be helping out in our classroom now. Isn't that nice?"

Nodding heads and a chorus of "yes" and "yea" welcomed Jolissa, and her stomach unclenched a little. She nodded and smiled her thanks, wanting to hold off speaking to them until she had no choice.

"Well, Miss Jolissa," Mrs. Feingold said, "I will leave you in capable hands and get back to my own work now." She offered a quick wave to the children. "Have a nice day, boys and girls!"

They waved and called good-bye in return, and then she was gone. Jolissa felt exposed and more than slightly awkward.

"Come sit down with us." Miss Ginny pulled another chair next to hers. "We're going to finish our story, and then we'll have our morning snack."

Jolissa swallowed and approached the group, about to lower herself into the chair when a little boy with huge brown eyes and dark curly hair pulled on her pant leg. Surprised, Jolissa looked down.

"Can I sit on your lap, Miss Jowissa?"

Unsure of proper protocol, she turned to the teacher, who nodded her approval. "That would be fine, if Miss Jolissa doesn't mind. But you'll all have to take turns, remember? And class, it's Miss Jo-*li*-ssa. Say it with me."

The class repeated her name several times, and then the little boy who had said it wrong climbed up on her lap. His head hung low, and she thought she knew exactly what he was feeling. She smiled when he snuggled up against her, and together they settled in to hear the rest of the story.

❋ ❋ ❋

"COME IN, COME IN!" *Abuela* swung the door wide and stepped back so Jolissa could enter. "How did it go? I want to hear all about your first day."

"I c-c-can't s-s-stay long." She walked into the entryway and was immediately greeted by a meowing, purring Mario. She picked him up and turned back to Eva, who closed the front door and led the way into the living room.

"This is l-l-later th-th-than I usually g-g-get off, and I h-h-have to g-g-get home and fix d-d-dinner before s-s-school, but—"

Abuela interrupted her as they settled down on opposite sides of the sofa, Mario quickly making himself at home on Jolissa's lap. "But you took the time to stop by and see your old *abuela* on the way home. I am so pleased. Now tell me. How was it?"

Jolissa's hand rested on the cat's fur, and his purring calmed her. "I . . . I w-w-was nervous, b-b-but I th-th-think it w-w-went OK." She smiled. "I m-m-made a new f-f-friend. His n-n-name is J-J-Jordan. H-h-he s-s-sat on my l-l-lap."

"Of course he did. You have such a kind and caring heart, and people sense that. Especially children."

"J-J-Jordan s-s-said it's OK th-th-that I t-t-talk f-f-funny because s-s-sometimes he does t-t-too." She chuckled. "He c-c-calls m-m-me 'Jowissa' because he j-j-j-just c-c-can't s-s-say Jolissa."

"There, you see? God has placed you in the perfect job. Children are so accepting. Before long they won't even notice that you stutter."

"Do y-y-you really th-th-think so?"

"Absolutely, *mija*. I hardly notice it myself unless you bring it up." She leaned forward. "And don't forget what the woman at church told me yesterday—that you didn't stutter before your parents died. God must have wanted you to know that for some reason."

A wave of hopelessness swept over her, nearly washing away the joy she'd felt only moments earlier. Was she kidding herself? Could she really and truly work effectively with children and help them in some way?

At the moment she knew she had no choice but to try. Her job at the cleaners was gone, and there weren't many other jobs out there, especially not for someone like her.

Someone like me. Tio would tell me I'm worthless—an idiota who can't do anything right. But Abuela doesn't seem to agree. And the people at the school are willing to at least give me a chance. What about You, God? What do You say about me? Can I do this? Will You help me?

Her heart skipped a beat as the answer seemed to echo from deep within herself. *I will never leave you. I have called you. You are Mine. I have good plans for your future. On your own you can do nothing, but through Me you can do all things.*

Tears popped into her eyes. "*Abuela*, I th-th-th-think God j-j-just s-s-spoke to m-m-me."

Eva smiled. "And what did He say, *mija?*"

"Th-th-that everything is g-g-going to b-b-be all r-r-right, that H-H-He's going to t-t-take c-c-care of m-m-me."

The old woman nodded. "Amen. And so He will."

※　※　※

By Wednesday, Jolissa was settling into her new job. She was also excited that her transfer request had been approved at school, and now she was free to regularly attend midweek services. The weather had been a bit drizzly when she stopped by Eva's to pick her up that evening, so they'd decided to drive rather than walk to church.

"Have you talked to your *tio* about the car yet?"

The service was over and they were heading home. Jolissa kept her eyes on the road as she answered. "N-n-not yet, *Abuela*. I know I sh-sh-should. I w-w-was going t-t-to the n-n-night I t-t-told him about m-m-my n-n-new job, b-b-but he g-g-got s-s-so upset I ch-ch-changed my m-m-mind."

"I understand, *mija*. There's no rush. God will let you know when the time is right."

Jolissa sighed. It was hard to imagine the time ever being right to tell *tio* such a thing, but she knew she should keep praying about it. She steered the car into the driveway and on past the house to the little garage in back.

"Do you have time to come in for a few minutes?"

Jolissa didn't have to be at work until nine the next morning, and she had to admit that she'd much prefer to come home after *Tío* had gone to bed for the night. "S-s-sure. I'd l-l-like that."

The two women set about making some hot tea, and *Abuela* even placed a few cookies on a plate. Within moments they had settled down at the kitchen table, the ever-present

Mario once again perched on Jolissa's lap.

"Your job is working out well so far, isn't it?" Eva held her steaming mug between her hands and watched Jolissa do the same.

Jolissa nodded. "Y-y-yes. I really l-l-love it. The k-k-kids are w-w-wonderful, and s-s-so is Miss G-Ginny and the other t-t-teachers too."

Abuela smiled. "I'm so pleased."

A pair of large dark eyes invaded her thoughts, and Jolissa frowned, setting her cup down in front of her. She shook her head. "I s-s-still keep th-th-thinking about the l-l-l-little girl wh-wh-who ended up in f-f-foster c-c-care. I w-w-wish I could h-h-have h-h-helped her."

Eva set her own cup down and reached out to lay her hand on Jolissa's. "Lupita. Yes, I know you do, *mija*. But remember, God had His purpose in letting you see her and sealing that memory to your heart so you could pray for her. You might not be able to help her directly, but you can help so many other little ones who need you just as much."

She forced a smile. "L-l-like J-J-Jordan. I l-l-love them all, b-b-but—"

"But he's your favorite."

Jolissa nodded again. "He's s-s-so s-s-sweet . . . and sh-sh-shy. I th-th-think w-w-we unders-st-stand each other."

"I'm sure you do." Eva withdrew her hand and took another sip of tea. "The Lord understands you too, *mija*. Better than you understand yourself. He knows your needs even before you do."

Jolissa raised her eyes and studied her *abuela*. What was she trying to tell her?

"Fanny Crosby knew that truth well. She'd been forced to learn it many times over." She smiled. "One time she needed five dollars, so she decided to pray and ask God to provide it. She'd scarcely finished praying when a stranger knocked on her door and said he'd stopped by because he admired her work and wanted to meet her. Before he left he handed her a five-dollar bill. She immediately sat down and began to write 'All the Way My Savior Leads Me.' That was in 1874."

The two women paused as they sipped their tea and allowed Eva's words to sink in. After a few moments the old woman continued. "Her most famous hymn is undoubtedly 'Blessed Assurance, Jesus Is Mine.' She wrote that in 1873 when one of her close friends came over to visit. Her friend told her she'd composed a melody and wanted to play it for Fanny on the piano. She did, and then she asked Fanny what the tune said to her. She quickly replied, 'Blessed Assurance, Jesus Is Mine.' And so one of the greatest gospel songs of all time was born."

"Each s-s-song h-h-has its own s-s-story," Jolissa observed.

Eva nodded. "One of my personal favorites is 'To God Be the Glory,' though it wasn't discovered until many years after Fanny wrote it. Someone introduced it to George Beverly Shea, with the Billy Graham Crusade, and when he and the choir sang it in Toronto in 1955, it was an immediate hit." She reached for a cookie and broke off a piece. "So you see, *mija*, things don't always happen when or how we think they should, and we may even think God has forgotten us, but in His perfect timing, it all comes together."

Jolissa swallowed. She loved the way her *abuela* told her stories about the amazing woman named Fanny Crosby and somehow found a way to make them personal.

"I'd b-b-better f-f-finish and get h-h-home." She smiled and took a final swig of her tea, wondering how all this new knowledge of the blind songwriter would one day play out in her own life.

Chapter 24

ONE OF THE CHILDREN had a birthday party on Friday, and Jolissa found herself nearly as excited as the students themselves.

The little girl's mother had brought the cupcakes in early that day, but Miss Ginny explained to the class that they would wait to eat them until midafternoon, after they'd all had time to digest their lunches. Jolissa watched the children eye the cupcakes, and she knew they longed to lick the pink icing off the top, even as she did.

Lunch came and went uneventfully, with the exception of one instance where one of the bigger boys in the class tried to confiscate someone else's juice drink. Jolissa watched closely to see how Miss Ginny would handle it. She stepped in quickly, returned the drink to its rightful owner before the other boy could open or taste it, and then explained to both of them how important it was to respect one another's possessions, whether toys or food or anything else. She then encouraged the juice culprit to apologize, which he did, and in minutes the two boys were chatting and laughing as they finished their lunch.

Then, at last, it was time for the party. The children took their seats around a low, oblong table. Small, individual water bottles were passed out to each child, with both Miss Ginny and Jolissa helping to open them. Finally the cupcakes were distributed, and Miss Ginny reminded the children that they should thank God before eating them. Jolissa was about to sit down too when Miss Ginny spoke. "Miss Jolissa, would you offer the prayer of thanks, please?"

Jolissa felt her eyes go wide. *Me? Pray . . . out loud?* Her heart raced and her stomach churned. *Please, God, You know I can't do this!*

Two small arms wrapped themselves around her leg, and she looked down to see Jordan leaning against her, his face peering upward. When their eyes met, he smiled. "Pray, Miss Jowissa?"

She swallowed. She no longer had a choice. *Help me, Lord!* "F-F-Father, th-th-thank Y-Y-You for th-th-this food and f-f-for Amber's b-b-birthday. Amen."

Her cheeks flamed, as she wondered if her prayer had been long enough or if she'd said the right things. At least no one laughed at the way she talked. They were far too busy licking frosting and peeling crinkled wrappers off their treats. Jolissa was so nervous she doubted she could eat anything, but with Jordan still at her side, they joined the others at the table.

❋ ❋ ❋

IT WAS THE PERFECT ENDING TO A PERFECT DAY—a perfect week, actually—and Jolissa couldn't be happier or more content. She and her *abuela* sat by the window in a quaint little eatery by the ocean, watching the sun set on the water and waiting for their food.

"It's lovely here, isn't it?"

Jolissa turned from the gorgeous view and smiled at her dinner companion. She wondered how a woman in her eighties could be so youthful, despite her wrinkles and graying hair. But there was no arguing the fact that she was.

"Y-y-yes, I l-l-love it. I'm s-s-so glad y-y-you t-t-talked me into th-th-this."

Eva laughed. "It wasn't easy."

Jolissa smiled. *Abuela* was right. When Jolissa arrived at Eva's house late that evening, immediately after fixing dinner for *Tio* and then leaving him alone to eat it—and hopefully to get over his especially foul mood—her *abuela* had told her she thought they should do something special to go out and celebrate.

"C-c-celebrate?" Jolissa had been confused. "Wh-wh-what w-w-will we b-b-be celebrating?"

Eva's eyes had sparkled. "Why, your new job, of course! And your new life in Jesus, above all else. This calls for something special, and I know just the place."

Jolissa had argued all the way from the house to the car and then on to the restaurant, insisting there was no need to do anything special just for her. But *Abuela* had argued right back that it was her treat in more ways than one. "I will pay for our celebration meal," she'd explained, "but it will also be a very special treat for me. I haven't been out to eat in months."

And now here they were. Jolissa couldn't help but think that her *abuela* may not have been out to eat in months, but Jolissa hadn't been out to eat since . . . she could scarcely remember when. *Tio* saw no reason to waste money on eating out when they had food at home.

Jolissa nodded. "Y-y-you are r-r-right. I'm g-g-glad y-y-you insisted. Th-th-this is w-w-wonderful."

"Wait till you taste the food. It's delicious! This place has been here for years." A flicker of sadness sparked in her eyes. "Guillermo and I came here once a week, just to watch the sunset and enjoy the food." She sighed. "It doesn't hurt as much now as when he first died, but I don't suppose you ever get over missing someone you love."

Her mouth drew into an *O* as she apparently realized what she'd said, and she laid her hand on Jolissa's arm. "I am so sorry, *mija*. I didn't mean to cause you pain. I know you must still miss your parents terribly."

Tears threatened as Jolissa nodded. "It's O-O-OK, *Abuela*. I know y-y-you didn't m-m-mean to h-h-hurt me. But y-y-yes, I s-s-still m-m-miss them."

"And you always will, so long as you're on this earth. But remember, you will see them again."

A slight smile dispelled the tears. "I'm s-s-so glad to know th-th-that."

The waitress came with two bowls of clam chowder and set them on the table, along with a small basket of warm bread. "Can I get you ladies anything else? More water?"

Eva and Jolissa shook their heads. "No, thank you," Eva said, smiling up at the woman, who returned the smile and walked away.

"Do you like clam chowder, *mija*?"

Jolissa's cheeks warmed. "I . . . d-d-don't know. I've n-n-never h-h-had it b-b-before."

Eva raised her eyebrows. "Well then, you're in for a treat." She reached over and took Jolissa's hand. "Would you offer thanks for our food? *Por favor, mija*. Please."

Her heart felt as if it had stopped. Pray out loud? Again? Twice in one day? Of all people, *Abuela* should realize how hard that was for her. But how could she say no, after all the dear old woman had done for her?

She bowed her head and closed her eyes. "D-d-dear L-L-Lord, thank You f-f-for this f-f-food and f-f-for my *abuela*—and f-f-for everything Y-Y-You've done for m-m-me. In Jesus' n-n-name, amen."

She lifted her head and her gaze to find *Abuela* smiling at her. "That was perfect, *mija*."

Perfect? It was short and full of stutters. How could it be perfect? But she decided not to ask, glad she had at least remembered this time to end the prayer "in Jesus' name," as she'd heard her *abuela* do so many times. She followed Eva's lead and tasted the soup.

Her eyes widened, and she looked over at *Abuela*. "Th-th-this is w-w-wonderful!"

Eva chuckled. "It is, isn't it? I knew you'd like it."

The sun dipped below the horizon then, and Jolissa turned to watch the skyline fade from blue to purple. The sunlight no longer sparkled on the water, but a sense of peace and rest had settled upon it. If only she could feel this way all the time—but of course, she knew she couldn't. No matter how nice her life was now with her new job and *Abuela*, there was still her *tio* to consider.

No. She shook off the thought and returned to her soup. She would go back to the reality of her life with *tio* later. For now she would enjoy her celebration dinner with the *abuela* God had given her. *Thank You, Lord*, she prayed, as the soup warmed and comforted her heart.

✳ ✳ ✳

SHE DROVE EVA BACK and parked the car in the garage before leaving immediately for home. *Abuela* had tried to convince her to come inside for a while, but she had forced herself to go, though she longed to stay. Eva had even urged her to take the car home and tell her *tio* about it, but her stomach clenched at the thought.

"I c-c-can't," she'd told her. "Not y-y-yet."

But when? The thought rolled around in her mind as she walked the few blocks toward home, threatening to steal the peace and joy she'd experienced at dinner. *When am I finally going to have the nerve to tell him about the car? What will he say? Will he let me have it? What will I do if refuses? I could insist, but . . .*

The thought drifted off and died where all thoughts of resistance died when it came to her *tio*. From the time she'd first come to live with him as a brokenhearted orphan-child, she'd known resistance was futile. And besides, she'd been too emotionally crushed even to consider trying. Instead she'd learned to live with verbal and emotional abuse as if it were a normal part of life.

But it's not, she told herself. *Just because I've survived it all these years doesn't mean it's right. I can tell that by being with* Abuela. *And the way Miss Ginny and the kids treat me at school . . . as if I were normal, like other people.*

She caught her breath as a silent response echoed in her heart. *You are My child, precious in My sight. I formed you in your mother's womb, exactly as I designed you to be—for My purposes.*

Jolissa turned the corner onto the street where she lived, nearly blinded by tears of joy. God had spoken to her—again! He loved her. He called her His child. And He had designed her exactly as He wanted her to be. It was almost more than she could absorb.

Her heart still soared as she unlocked the front door and stepped inside. She heard the TV blaring and walked toward the living room, only slightly concerned that her *tio* had waited up for her. She'd hoped he would be asleep already, but she was certain that even one of his angry outbursts couldn't steal her joy at this moment.

Then she saw him, slumped over in his chair, his head lolling to the side. So he was asleep after all. *Strange. I've never known* Tio *to fall asleep like that. When he gets tired he always goes to bed.*

She approached his chair, frowning as she bent closer to his face. His color wasn't right, and she couldn't hear his breathing. Trembling, she touched his shoulder. "T-T-Tio?"

He didn't move. She held her hand in front of his mouth but felt no puffs of air. When she laid her hand against his neck, she could scarcely feel a pulse. "*Tio!*" She grabbed his shoulder, tighter this time, and shook. "*T-T-Tio,* w-w-wake up!"

When he still didn't respond, she raced to the kitchen and grabbed the phone. She dialed 911 and waited. Thankfully the operator answered quickly.

"It's m-m-my *t-t-tio.* M-m-my uncle. S-s-s-something's wrong w-w-with him. He's in h-h-his wh-wh-wheelchair, b-b-but—"

"Calm down, ma'am. Take it slow, and tell me what's happening."

Drawing in a deep breath, Jolissa did her best to stumble through a brief explanation. At last the operator assured her that help was on the way, and she hung up to return to her *tio's* side. Oh, if only she knew some sort of CPR! But she didn't, so she knelt down beside the chair and took his hand in hers. "*Tio,*" she whispered. "*T-T-Tio.*"

The thought occurred to her then that instead of trying to speak to her uncle, she needed to pray. Should she call *Abuela? Later,* she decided. *Prayer first.*

"Help h-h-him, L-L-Lord," she prayed aloud, oblivious to her stuttering. "D-d-don't l-l-let my *t-t-tio* die. He d-d-doesn't even know Y-Y-You! S-s-save him, Father, p-p-please!"

The distant wail of a siren assured her that human help was on the way, but she knew it wouldn't be enough. Her uncle needed the Lord's help, and she was going to continue to pray for him for as long as it took.

Chapter 25

THE AMBULANCE HAD WHISKED JOLISSA'S *TIO* away before she realized she'd have to call a cab or walk several miles to get to the hospital. Instead she'd called Eva and then raced to her house. Her *abuela* had said the car was hers to use any time she wished, and this was one of those times. Eva was ready and waiting for her when she arrived.

"Come, *mija*," she said, her purse already hanging on her arm when she opened the front door. "I'll go with you."

They were in the car and heading for the emergency room within minutes. Jolissa reminded herself not to speed, wondering all the while why she was so concerned about her uncle's condition.

His salvation, she reminded herself. *He doesn't know Jesus as his Savior. As cruel as he's been to me over the years, I can't bear the thought of him ending up in hell.* But deep down she knew it was more than that.

"I have been praying ever since you called." Eva patted Jolissa's arm. "I know you have too."

Jolissa nodded. "Y-y-yes, I d-d-don't w-w-want him to d-d-die without r-r-receiving Jesus."

"Of course you don't. Neither do I." Her voice dropped a notch. "And neither does God, *mija*. He loves him more than we do, you know."

Love *Tio?* God, yes. She could accept that He loved everyone, just because . . . well, because He was God. But . . .

"I . . . I d-d-don't know if I l-l-love *T-T-Tio.*" She felt the shame burn in her cheeks and was glad *Abuela* couldn't see it in the darkness.

"Ah, *mija*, of course you do. I heard it in your voice when you called me and told me what happened." She sighed. "You know, we can love someone without approving of their actions or behavior. We don't even have to like them. But we do have to love them—even your *tio.* He's made in God's image, you know, just as you and I are. And Jesus died for him."

Abuela's words echoed in her heart and rolled around in her mind. She could think of nothing to say, and she was glad when *Abuela* continued speaking.

"You think you don't love him because you believe love is about feelings. It's not, you know. It's about actions. You showed your love for your *tio* when you called 911 and when you began praying for him. That's the sort of love he needed at that moment. You didn't let him down. You loved him just the way Jesus wanted you to."

A threat of tears loomed, but she quickly blinked them back. She was driving and had to get them to the hospital safely. "Th-th-thank you, *Abuela.*" Her voice cracked as she spoke, and the two women rode the remaining few blocks in silence.

❉ ❉ ❉

"I WISH I'D THOUGHT TO BRING THE QUILT." Eva's comment came after they'd spent several hours in the waiting room, praying, sitting, pacing, making small talk, . . . and praying some more. Jolissa had filled out the necessary paperwork for her uncle's admission and had spoken with a doctor once after that, who explained they were taking Joseph into surgery. They'd heard nothing since.

"That w-w-would have b-b-been nice." She smiled at her *abuela*'s thoughtfulness.

"Of course, we don't need the quilt to talk about Fanny's story. I can tell you a little more about her songs, and then next time we'll start on a new patch. Would you like that, *mija*?"

Jolissa nodded. "Th-th-that would b-b-be a g-g-good thing r-r-right n-n-n-now. Th-th-thank you, *Abuela*."

"I thought so." Eva's smile was warm, her eyes tender. "It will help you get your mind off your uncle, at least for a few minutes. And it will be good for you to be reminded of God's faithfulness in someone else's life." She leaned across the small space between their plastic chairs and added, "Because He loves you just as much as He loved Fanny Crosby, you know."

Jolissa's mind agreed with that statement, but her heart continued to wrestle with a truth that seemed so foreign to the way she pictured herself. After all, Fanny Crosby was a courageous woman who did amazing things. She was quite obviously gifted by God, and she used her gift in powerful ways. How could someone like Jolissa compare to such a heroic woman of faith?

"Let me think now, about some of Fanny's other songs I haven't told you about yet." Eva drew her brows together and paused for a moment. Then her face lit up and she smiled and nodded. "Yes, one of my favorite stories is about 'Saved by Grace,' which Fanny wrote in 1891. She was seventy-one years old then, but still writing and speaking every chance she got. She had attended a prayer meeting and heard a man speak on the Twenty-third Psalm. His subject was grace. Later that same week he died, and Fanny found herself wondering about what the man was experiencing now that he had left his temporal life on earth behind. She then considered her own death and wondered about her first impression of heaven. The answer came to her, and she declared, 'Why, my eyes will be opened and I will see my Saviour face-to-face.' When she was asked a few days later to write a hymn about grace, she sat down and penned the words to 'Saved by Grace.' You see, *mija*, God can use anything in our lives—and even in our death—to bless others."

Encouraged, Jolissa nodded, waiting for Eva to continue.

"She wrote so many songs during her lifetime, and I know I could never name them all. But one I dearly love is 'I Am Thine, O Lord,' which came about after a conversation she'd had with a friend regarding the nearness of God. 'Jesus, Keep Me Near the Cross' is another beautiful hymn, and she wrote that simply because a gentleman said he wanted a new song to sing at an evangelistic service that night. And 'Savior, More than Life to Me' was written when that same gentleman requested a song on the theme of every day and hour."

She shrugged. "So you see, *mija*, some hymns came about as a result of some major happening in Fanny's life; others were written simply because they needed to be. God gave her the words when the time was right."

Jolissa took her *abuela*'s hand and squeezed it. "Th-th-thank you f-f-for t-t-telling me these s-s-stories."

Eva nodded. "We will start on a new patch and another aspect of Fanny's life next time you are at my house. For now, would you like to pray again?"

"Y-y-yes, please. I w-w-would."

✳ ✳ ✳

THE SUN WAS BEGINNING to light the eastern sky, rising slowly above the mountaintops as a weary Jolissa steered

Eva's car toward home. Her *abuela* had convinced her to come and stay with her until her uncle got out of the hospital, and she had readily agreed, having dreaded the idea of staying at home alone. They'd stopped there long enough to pick up a few things Jolissa would need, and they were now only a block of so from Eva's place.

"I know y-y-you are t-t-tired, *Abuela*." Jolissa snuck a peek at the elderly woman, whose wrinkles seemed deeper than they had the day before.

Her smile was weak. "I'm fine, *mija*. I just need some sleep . . . and so do you."

Jolissa knew Eva was right. Her own shoulders ached and her eyes felt as if they were weighed down with sand. She could only imagine how someone in her eighties must feel after being up all night.

"But at least we know your *tio* will be all right."

Abuela's reassurance seemed a bit premature to Jolissa, since the doctor had simply said her uncle had come through the surgery successfully and would be released from CCU to a regular room once they were certain he was out of danger and on the road to recovery.

Jolissa frowned as she pulled into the driveway and drove past the house to the garage. "The d-d-doctor s-s-said his arteries w-w-were clogged. They c-c-cleared them, but h-h-he has t-t-to eat healthier f-f-foods. H-h-how will I m-m-make him d-d-do that?"

Eva chuckled. "It won't be easy, *mija*, but all you can do is try. You can't make him do anything. But we will pray he will listen to the doctor's advice and not fight you about it."

Jolissa shut off the engine and turned toward Eva. "Do y-y-you th-th-think it was m-m-my fault? I'm th-th-the one who f-f-fixes his m-m-meals."

"No, *mija*." Eva shook her head and reached out to take Jolissa's hand. "It is not your fault. You must never talk that way. I've heard you say you fix him salad and vegetables whenever you can, but that sometimes he refuses to eat them. He likes his tortillas and fried meats and desserts. And it won't be easy to get him to change his habits."

"My *t-t-tio* does not l-l-listen to me. He w-w-will yell at m-m-me if I argue w-w-with him."

Eva squeezed her hand. "And that is why we will pray about his attitude. Remember, *mija*, nothing is too hard for God—not even your *tio*'s heart."

Jolissa smiled. She wanted so much to believe her *abuela*'s words, but right now she wanted sleep even more. "L-l-let's g-g-go inside. I'm s-s-so tired, and I know y-y-you are t-t-too."

"I won't deny that. My bed is calling me, though I will have to put out some fresh food and water for Mario first."

"I'll d-d-do that, *Abuela*. Y-y-you j-j-just go to b-b-bed. I'll c-c-call the h-h-hospital too and g-g-give them y-y-your number in c-c-case th-th-they need to t-t-talk to m-m-me."

Eva agreed and headed straight down the hallway toward her room the moment they walked through the kitchen door. Jolissa stopped and picked up a meowing Mario and comforted him as she filled his bowls. Then she made her call and went straight to the spare room, where she collapsed on the soft double bed where the singing quilt lay folded at the bottom. Jolissa smiled when she saw it, knowing that its usual place was in Eva's room. No doubt her *abuela* had instead placed it on the bed in the spare room at God's direction. The thought comforted her as she drifted off into a much-needed sleep.

Chapter 26

IT WAS SLIGHTLY AFTER NOON on Saturday by the time Eva awoke to the muted sounds of someone puttering around in the kitchen. She had to pull her thoughts into focus before she remembered that Jolissa had come home with her after their long night at the hospital. She hoped the girl had gotten some sleep.

Eva stretched and rolled over, surprised that Mario wasn't beside her, as he usually was in the morning. She smiled. The cat could be fickle when he wanted to be, but in this case she knew he simply loved Jolissa—as did she.

She closed her eyes. "Good morning, Father," she whispered, reticent to climb out from under the covers just yet. "Thank You for the beautiful sunlight shining through my window. Thank You for this lovely home You've blessed me with, and for a new granddaughter who is now Your daughter as well. I have so much to be grateful for, Lord, and I am. Please, Father, help me today to be a blessing to others, especially Jolissa and her *tio*. Oh Lord, please rescue that man. Save him, Father, as You saved me—by Your great mercy and grace. I deserve hell, *El Señor*, but by Your great mercy I am spared that fate. And I certainly do not deserve heaven, but by Your grace I will spend eternity there, in Your presence." She shook her head. "Even after all these years, Father, it is still almost too much to comprehend. But I know it's true because of the promises in Your Word and because of Your sweet presence in my life. Thank You. Thank You, my Lord and my Savior."

Slowly Eva opened her eyes and threw the covers back, then sat up and eased her legs over the side, fumbling for her slippers with her feet. Soft and well-worn, the slippers slid into place, and then she reached for her robe at the end of the bed. A nice cup of coffee with Jolissa sounded like a perfect way to start the day. Then she imagined they would head back to the hospital to check on Uncle Joseph.

She smiled at the name. Joseph in the Bible, the betrothed of Mary, the mother of Jesus, was a kind and gentle man, fair and strong and patient. Would the angry old man who had spent the majority of his life in a wheelchair ever begin to live up to his name?

* * *

JOLISSA SAT ON A COLD METAL FOLDING CHAIR beside her *tio*'s bed, listening to the bleeps of the attached machines and watching the numbers flash on the screen, monitoring his vital signs. He was still in CCU, but the nurse had assured her that the doctor had said if Joseph continued to improve, they would move him to a regular room the following day. Relief had washed over her at the news, and she found herself thanking God even as she watched her uncle's chest rise and fall. His eyes were shut, but his color was better than when she'd found him the night before. What if she hadn't come home when she did? She shuddered to think of the outcome if he'd died there all alone.

Thank You, Lord, that You didn't let that happen. Thank You for taking care of my tio. *Please help him to turn to You, Father. He needs You.*

She knew she could stay only a few minutes longer, as visitation time was severely limited in CCU. There would be more time to visit tomorrow when they moved him to another room. The thought stirred up mixed emotions inside her.

It's easier to visit with him this way, Lord—when he can't hear me or speak to me. But what about tomorrow? What's going to happen when he starts getting better and finds out he can't eat the way he wants to anymore? How am I ever going to make him take care of himself?

For an instant she thought a large hand had been placed on her shoulder, and she nearly turned around to see who it was. Then she heard the voice. *Be still, daughter. I will take care of everything. Tomorrow is not your concern. Rest now.*

"Th-th-thank You, F-F-Father," she whispered. "Thank Y-Y-You for t-t-taking c-c-care of my *t-t-tio*."

As the hand lifted from her shoulder, she raised her gaze to find her uncle staring at her. When their eyes met, he closed his and turned away.

❋ ❋ ❋

"So, church tomorrow morning. Are you looking forward to it, *mija*?"

Jolissa stood at the stove, stirring soup for a quick supper. She turned to look at Eva, who waited at the kitchen table. Jolissa was glad that her *abuela* had finally begun to let her help with fixing meals and cleaning up afterward. She was also pleased to see that Mario had taken up residence on Eva's lap. She smiled at the picture they made together.

"Y-y-yes, I t-t-truly am. It's b-b-been a hard w-w-week-end so f-f-far."

Eva nodded. "Indeed it has." She smiled. "But your *tio* is going to be fine. By tomorrow he should be out of CCU and in his own room. Then all we have to do is convince him to take better care of himself."

Jolissa nearly laughed out loud. "I'm g-g-glad y-y-you said *w-w-we*. I'm g-g-going to n-n-need all the h-h-help I can g-g-get to m-m-make that h-h-happen."

"And you shall have it. You know I'll continue to pray, and we both know that God hears us and He loves us—and He loves *Tio* Joseph. I believe we shall see evidence of that very soon."

"I'm just g-g-grateful He s-s-saved *T-T-Tio's* life. Now we m-m-must p-p-pray that his s-s-soul is s-s-saved too."

"We have done what we can, *mija*. We have prayed and will continue to do so, and now we do as the Bible says— stand still and see God's salvation."

Jolissa turned back to the stove, giving the soup a final stir before ladling it into bowls. She desperately wanted to believe her *abuela*, but imagining her *tio* saved—loving and worshipping God? It was almost too much to grasp.

Did you deserve to be saved? Do you deserve to be My child?

Quickly she set the bowls back down on the counter, afraid she would spill them if she didn't. The questions had pierced her heart with their truth. Of course she didn't deserve to be saved or to be God's child. Why, then, would she think God required anything different of her *tio*?

Taking a deep breath, she prayed that God would steady her hands and then carried the soup to the table.

Chapter 27

SUPPER WAS OVER and Eva sensed that it was time to get back to Fanny's story before they went to bed. As Jolissa washed the few dishes that were in the sink, Eva retrieved the quilt.

"Are you ready to learn more about the amazing queen of gospel songs, *mija*?"

Jolissa dried her hands and rejoined her *abuela* at the table. "I r-r-really am. How d-d-did you know?"

Eva smiled and held up the portion of the quilt with the musical note. "Before we finish the huge part of Fanny's story that revolves around her poems and hymns, you should know that she also wrote several political songs and even participated in the writing of three cantatas. But her heart was always in her songs that gave honor and worship to God."

"That's th-th-the m-m-most important."

"Yes, it is, and Fanny knew that very well." She rearranged the quilt so she could once again point out the patch with the cross on it. "But whatever she did, she knew it all revolved around her relationship to Christ. From that central point she never deviated."

Eva paused as Mario stood and stretched himself, then hopped from her lap to the floor before hopping right back up, this time onto Jolissa's lap. When he had arranged himself once again, she continued.

"As I've mentioned to you before, Fanny often spoke at rescue missions, churches, and even prisons. And though most people think of her as a hymn writer, she considered herself primarily a rescue mission worker. She loved working with society's castoffs, the downtrodden and homeless, anyone in need, including immigrants who had come to this country with high hopes, only to end up starving and unable to find jobs. She never tired of working as long or hard as she could to try to help them. She and her husband often took part in organizing concerts so they could raise money to give to the poor." She shook her head. "Throughout her life, even when she received income for her writing, Fanny Crosby seldom had a dime to her name. She gave away almost everything the moment she recognized a need."

"She w-w-was a very k-k-kind and l-l-loving w-w-woman."

Eva smiled and extended her hand to cover Jolissa's. "She reminds me of you, *mija*."

Jolissa's eyes grew wide. "Oh, n-n-no, *Abuela*. Sh-sh-she w-w-was much m-m-more d-d-dedicated and g-g-gifted."

She patted the young woman's hand. "Don't sell yourself short. You haven't even begun to see what God has planned for you." Eva pointed to the patch with the quill. "Remember this one, *mija*? I showed it to you when I started telling you about the many songs Fanny wrote— and we haven't even scratched the surface of the thousands she penned. But this writing quill represents more than individual poems and songs. Besides the book I mentioned that she wrote as a young student, *The Blind Girl, and Other Poems*, she wrote several other books."

Eva closed her eyes for a moment. "Let me see how many titles I can remember. There was *Monterey and Other Poems, A Wreath of Columbia's Flowers, Bells at Evening and Other Poems*, and *Memories of Eighty Years*." She opened her eyes and chuckled. "No doubt when she wrote her book of memories she thought she was at the end of her life. As it turned out she had another decade to go. And as much as she was able, she stayed active right up to the end."

"H-h-how old w-w-was she wh-wh-when she d-d-died?"

"Ninety-four, nearly ninety-five." Eva nodded. "Yes, almost ninety-five years, nearly all of them devoted to serving God. Isn't that a wonderful legacy? And oh, how she was loved! The church was packed for her funeral, where the choir sang her favorite song, 'Faith of Our Fathers.' Of course, they sang many of her own songs as well, including 'Safe in the Arms of Jesus' and 'Saved by Grace.' Her minister summed up her life when he said, 'There must have been a royal welcome when this queen of sacred song burst the bonds of death and passed into the glories of heaven.' I imagine there wasn't a dry eye in the building by that time."

Jolissa's eyes shone with her own tears. "I r-r-remember the f-f-funeral for my p-p-parents. I th-th-think that's wh-wh-where I m-m-might have h-h-heard 'B-B-Blessed Assurance' b-b-before."

Tears popped into Eva's eyes as she caught a glimpse of how expansively God was using this story of Fanny Crosby to minister to Jolissa's broken heart. *Thank You for letting me be part of this*, she prayed silently.

She set down the quilt so she could pull the little book from her pocket. "I brought this so I could read something else to you." She cleared her throat. "This was read at Fanny's funeral, the last verse of a poem written by another poet of the time, Eliza Edmunds Hewitt:

Good-bye, dearest Fanny, goodbye for a while,
You walk in the shadows no more;
Around you, the sunbeams of glory will smile;
The Lamb is the light of that Shore!"

Eva closed the book and lifted her gaze to meet Jolissa's. "A child, blind almost from birth, grew up to accomplish so much in her life because she trusted the One who held her in His nail-scarred hand. A quote on her tombstone reads simply, 'She hath done what she could!' But even that is only true because she knew her beloved Savior was using her for His glory." She watched the war of emotions play across Jolissa's face. "He will do the same for you, *mija*."

She folded the quilt, patted Jolissa's hand one last time, and then pulled herself to her feet. It was time to go to bed. She took a few steps and then stopped, turned around, and placed the quilt on the table in front of Jolissa. "I believe God wants you to have this, *mija*."

The young woman's mouth dropped open as if she wanted to speak but couldn't. Instead, she shook her head, as if silently refusing the gift.

Eva smiled. "It's not mine to keep or give away, nor yours to accept or refuse. It's God's gift to you. He wants you to have it. No arguments, *mija*. Good night."

✳ ✳ ✳

THE SUN SHONE BRIGHTLY overhead as Jolissa and Eva stepped out of the church doors and walked down the steps toward the parking lot. Jolissa had maintained a silent prayer vigil over her *tio* off and on throughout the night and even during the morning service. Now, as the two of them left to grab a quick lunch on the way to the hospital, she sensed a peace about her uncle's condition.

Thank You. Her silent prayer lifted her heart, and her step felt almost light. Whatever happened, she knew things would be all right. Look what Fanny Crosby had gone through in her lifetime, and yet God used her in ways Jolissa could only begin to imagine and appreciate. Though she was certain she'd never accomplish anything close to the things Fanny had done, the thought did give Jolissa hope for the future.

The two women stopped at the information table just inside the hospital entrance to inquire of Joseph's whereabouts and condition.

The volunteer at the desk scanned her records and smiled. "Yes, your uncle has been moved to his own room." She gave them the number. "The notation reads 'limited visitation.' That means you can both go on up to visit him, but don't wear him out. He's been through a lot and has a long way to go. Rest is the best thing for him."

"*Mija*, this is wonderful news!" Eva clasped Jolissa's arm as they headed for the elevator. "I'll be praying while you visit with your *tio*."

Jolissa's heart skipped. "You're n-n-not going w-w-with me?"

The old woman's eyes smiled. "No, *mija*. The visit is for you to do. My job is to pray while the two of you talk."

"But wh-wh-what if h-h-he gets upset and y-y-yells, or—"

"That's why I will be praying. Just relax, *mija*. It's going to be all right."

Jolissa wanted to believe her *abuela*, but years of experience with her *tio* made it difficult.

At last *Abuela* was settled into a chair in the small waiting room a few doors down from *Tio*'s room. Bible in hand, she shooed Jolissa off, assuring her she would be praying the entire time. With no other option in sight, Jolissa approached the open door of her *tio*'s room.

Her first thought was that there were nearly as many whooshing and beeping machines surrounding her *tio* as there had been when he was still in CCU. And he was still sleeping—a relief for the moment. She was also relieved that it was a private room. She couldn't imagine having this confrontation—which is what she still imagined it would become—with witnesses.

She eased her way to the side of his bed with the least trays and machines beside it. Telling herself she should say something, she opened her mouth and tried, but then decided there was no point since he was asleep. Instead she stood there, praying, until she sensed God whisper that she should take his hand.

Her legs nearly went out from under her at the thought. In all the years she'd lived with her *tio*, never once had they held hands or even touched unless it was absolutely necessary or accidental. *I can't do this, Lord. I can't!*

I know that. But I can.

His words were both a comfort and a challenge, for now she had no excuse. She glanced around and spotted a green plastic chair in the corner. Retrieving it, she pulled it up beside the bed and eased herself down into it. At least she wouldn't have to be dependent on her knees to hold her up.

Trembling, she reached toward her *tio*'s left hand, the one nearest her and without the inserted IV tube. His skin felt cool, and she was amazed at the smoothness of his skin.

"T-T-Tio." She was scarcely able to force the word from her dry throat. "*Tio*, it's m-m-me. J-J-Jolissa."

His eyes remained closed, but she felt his hand twitch. Had he heard her?

"T-T-Tio?"

His eyes opened just a slit. His head didn't move, but she saw his eyes slide in her direction. Her heart felt frozen in place.

"I'm h-h-here." She swallowed. Would he call her an *idiota* for making such an obvious statement? Even if he couldn't say it, she imagined he was thinking it.

Neither of them spoke. She waited, picturing her *abuela* praying and hoping God was listening. Should she say something? Sit quietly and wait? Maybe she should just leave.

"Jo . . . lissa."

The word was scarcely recognizable, but she realized it was the first time she'd ever heard him say it unless he was forced to introduce her to someone. He'd never addressed her by anything but *idiota* for as long as she could remember.

"Y-y-yes, *Tio*." She leaned closer, wondering if he might try to say something else. "I'm h-h-here."

"You . . . came for . . . me."

She frowned. What did he mean?

"You came . . . in time. You saved . . . me."

Hot tears bit her eyes, and brushed at them with her free hand. "Yes, *T-T-Tio*. I f-f-found you in y-y-your ch-ch-chair. I w-w-was so s-s-scared." The tears spilled over onto her cheeks then, and she couldn't wipe them away fast enough.

"Don't cry. I'm . . . not . . . worth it."

Jolissa's heart squeezed. "*Tio*, wh-wh-what do y-y-you mean? Of c-c-course you're w-w-worth it. I l-l-love y-y-you!" She gasped. What had she just said? Was it true? Did she really love the man who had raised her since her parents died, even though he'd never once spoken a kind word to her?

Tears pooled in Joseph's dark eyes. "You . . . never told me that . . . before."

I didn't know . . . until now. She bit her tongue to keep the thought from popping out. It might be true, but she doubted he needed to hear it at that moment. Instead she said, "You're my *t-t-tio*. Of course I l-l-love you."

She thought she detected a slight nod before he spoke again. "And I . . . I love you . . . *mija*."

Jolissa's mind reeled. She couldn't decide if she was more shocked that her uncle had used the word *love* or that he'd called her *mija*. The endearment came so naturally from her *abuela*, but from *Tio*? What could have happened to cause him to speak to her in such a way?

She had nearly worked up the nerve to ask him when a nurse came in and told her she'd need to let her uncle rest now. "You can see him again in a couple of hours. We don't want to wear him out. He's still very weak."

Jolissa nodded. She knew the nurse was right, but her heart longed to know more about this strange behavior from a man who had spent the last fourteen years berating and belittling her.

She squeezed his hand. "I'll b-b-be back after y-y-you get s-s-some rest."

Another nearly imperceptible nod, and then Joseph's eyes drifted closed. She would have to wait to learn anything more.

✹ ✹ ✹

"I D-D-DON'T KNOW WH-WH-WHAT TO TH-TH-THINK, *Abuela*. It's l-l-like he's s-s-s-somebody else."

Eva's face glowed as she listened to Jolissa recount her brief visit with her *tio*. "We are praying, *mija*, *sí?* Then we must believe that God is listening and answering."

Jolissa knew *Abuela* was right, but she still felt as if she'd been plucked right out of reality and dropped into some fantasy world, where ogres turned into kind and gentle people. Yes, yes, she knew that God had forgiven her and accepted her into His family, and He had reminded her that He would do no less for her *tio*. And yet, as silly as she knew it sounded, she wanted to ask God if He had ever met her *tio*, if He knew the kind of man he was.

Another ludicrous question. God, of course, knew her uncle far better than she did, but her mind just couldn't seem to wrap itself around the words her *tio* had spoken to her. And seeing tears in his eyes had nearly knocked her to the floor! Never, in all the fourteen years she'd lived with him, had she seen him cry, or even come close. The only explanation she could come up with was that God's love and power were so much bigger than anything she could imagine or comprehend.

"*Mija*, did you hear me?"

Her *abuela*'s words, as they sat in the hospital cafeteria, drinking coffee and waiting until Jolissa could visit her *tio* again, jolted her back to the present.

"I'm s-s-sorry, *Abuela*. What d-d-did y-y-you s-s-s-say?"

Eva smiled and patted Jolissa's hand. "I said that God is listening to our prayers and that He is at work in your *tio*'s heart and life."

Jolissa nodded. It had to be true. There simply was no other explanation—none at all.

Chapter 28

"I c-c-can't s-s-stay long, *T-T-Tio*. The n-n-nurse said f-f-fifteen minutes."

Joseph nodded. "Sit." Even whispered, his word became a command. She obeyed, pulling the plastic chair closer to his bed and lowering herself into it.

"We must talk." His dark eyes looked more alert now, and Jolissa wondered if possibly he had been under the effects of medication when he was kind to her earlier. Was he now reverting to his usual self?

She waited, her heart thrumming against her ribs.

"You said you loved me." The words weren't loud, but they were firm. "How is that possible?"

Jolissa raised her eyebrows and spoke the only words that came to mind. "Y-y-you're my *t-t-tio*."

He shook his head. "No. That's not enough reason. I am your *tio*, yes, but I have not treated you well. I know that, and I . . ." His expression softened. "I am ashamed. I do not deserve your love."

She scrambled for the right words, but none came. He spoke the truth; he had not treated her well. He did not deserve her love. *Help me, Lord!*

The answer came softly. *You do not deserve Mine, yet I poured it out for you on a painful, bloody cross.*

A flood of tears pricked her eyes, and she caught her breath, a vision of Christ being crucified etched into her mind. At that moment, she had her answer.

"L-l-love isn't earned, *T-T-Tio*. It's j-j-just freely r-r-received . . . b-b-because it's f-f-freely g-g-given." She swallowed. "G-G-God offered me H-H-His l-l-love, and I r-r-received it. I c-c-c-could n-n-never earn it."

His dark eyes studied her as she waited. At last he spoke. "Would He give it to me too . . . His love, I mean?"

Jolissa felt her eyes go wide, as the tears spilled over onto her cheeks and her heart rate accelerated. "If y-y-you ask H-H-Him. He w-w-will f-f-forgive you and g-g-give you H-H-His love if y-y-you j-j-just ask."

Again, he watched her for a moment, then closed his eyes. "Forgive me, God. I don't deserve Your love, but I . . . I need it. Please help me."

Her tears flowed freely now as, once again, she took her *tio*'s hand in hers. He opened his eyes and a flicker of a smile crossed his lips. "I believe God has forgiven me, but . . . can you?" Weakly, he squeezed her hand. "Please, *mija*."

The spoken endearment broke her heart, and she laid her head on his hand as she wept. "Yes, *T-T-Tio*," she sobbed. "I f-f-forgive y-y-y-you. I . . . f-f-forgive you."

She felt the release in her heart as she spoke the words, and she realized their relationship had crossed over from the pain of the past to the possibilities of the future. She could hardly wait to tell her *abuela* so they could rejoice together.

✳ ✳ ✳

"Miss Jowissa, it's Monday!"

The excitement in Jordan's dark eyes mirrored the joy Jolissa felt in her heart when she walked into the classroom that morning. She'd called the hospital before leaving *Abuela*'s house that morning and found that her *tio* had slept well during the night and was continuing to improve. She planned to go see him as soon as she got off work that afternoon.

"Yes, it is. You look excited about that, Jordan."

"That's 'cause I get to see you for five days!"

Jolissa chuckled and bent down to pick him up. "Well, that's a very good reason to be excited, isn't it?" She snuggled close until he pushed back and looked into her face, his forehead scrunched into a frown.

"What happened to you, Miss Jowissa?"

His question brought a frown to her brow. "What do you mean, Jordan?"

"You're not talking funny anymore."

She sucked in her breath. She still wasn't sure what he meant. She started to ask him, and then stopped. Though she had a hard time believing it, she realized she knew exactly what Jordan meant. She was no longer stuttering!

Her mind raced backward. When had this started? Surely not last night or *Abuela* would have commented on it. Jolissa had left for work early this morning, before Eva got up, so other than her phone call to the hospital, this was the first time she'd spoken to anyone since the previous evening.

"You're right, Jordan. I . . . don't talk funny anymore." She smiled at him, her eyes once again filling with tears. "I don't talk funny anymore!"

He eyed her suspiciously, as if wondering why she didn't realize that he was the one who had pointed this new development out to her. His expression reminded her of a puzzled old man, and she laughed out loud before planting a kiss on the top of his head.

"Thank you for telling me that," she said, easing his look of concern. "I am so glad you told me."

She set him down, but he continued to gaze up at her and follow her about the room as she talked to Miss Ginny and the other students. Each time Jolissa turned around, her little shadow was right behind her. Soon it was storytime, and they settled in to listen, with Jordan quickly crawling up into her lap. He smiled at her and patted her cheek, then laid his head against Jolissa's shoulder as Miss Ginny began to read.

✳ ✳ ✳

ON WEDNESDAY MORNING, while Jolissa and Eva sipped coffee before she had to leave for work, the hospital called to tell Jolissa her uncle was ready to come home. She hung up the phone and turned to her *abuela*, wide-eyed, her heart already beginning to race.

"They want me to pick up *Tío* this afternoon. They say he's ready to come home."

Eva's face brightened. "That's wonderful news, *mija*! Why do you look so worried?"

Jolissa sank back into the chair next to her *abuela*. "But . . . do you think he's ready? Isn't he still sick . . . and weak? He'll need me to take care of him. What about work? What should I do? Do you think they'd let me take off for a while? I just started last week, and—"

Abuela held up her hand to interrupt. "Hush, *mija*. It's all going to work out. I'm sure we can get a visiting nurse to stop by during the day for a while to check on his medical needs. And while you're at work, I'll stay with him. I can get him some soup or something to drink or . . . whatever he needs. Then when you get home, you can take over. It will be fine, *mija*. You'll see. I'll go with you this afternoon to pick him up."

"But, *Abuela*—"

"The discussion is closed, the plans are made, and you need to go to work." She smiled. "I'll be ready and waiting when you get home. Now go. You don't want to be late."

Jolissa swallowed, her mind reeling. So much had changed in such a short time, and God had been at the center of it all. Why should she believe He would abandon them now?

She sighed. "You're right. You are absolutely right." She stood up and started to walk away, then turned back and brushed a quick kiss on the old woman's forehead. "*Gracias, Abuela*. You are so good to me."

Eva looked up, her eyes glistening. "Not half as good as our Father is to both of us."

Jolissa nodded and smiled, and then turned and walked from the room.

Chapter 29

"*ABUELA*, DO YOU THINK IT'S A MIRACLE?"

Jolissa posed the question as they drove to the hospital to pick up her *tio*. It was a question she'd considered many times the past few days, one that even her uncle had asked about a couple days earlier.

"That you don't stutter anymore? Of course it's a miracle, *mija*. It's a good thing, yes? And the Bible says all good things come from God the Father—even though we don't deserve any of them. So yes, it is a miracle." She sighed. "But always, the greatest miracle of all is when God translates someone from the kingdom of darkness into the kingdom of His dear Son. Never forget that, *mija*. It is the greatest miracle any of us will ever experience or witness on this earth."

She knew her *abuela* was right. Still, she had another question. "Miss Ginny and I talked about it yesterday, and she said it's probably because I was able to forgive my *tio*, even after the way he treated me all these years."

"And no doubt that had a lot to do with it, but that doesn't make it any less a miracle. In fact, that you could forgive him at all and even realize that you have love for him is yet another miracle, don't you think?"

Jolissa nodded. "You're right, *Abuela*. I had no idea all the feelings I had stuffed down inside me until God used you to help bring them to the surface."

"I'm honored to be a part of it, *mija*. I'm always honored—and very humbled—that God uses me at all."

In less than an hour the paperwork was completed for Joseph's release from the hospital, and Jolissa could read the anticipation in his eyes as he sat in his wheelchair once again, ready to be rolled from his room to the exit. She and Eva stood ready to accompany him, as a hospital employee took his position behind the wheelchair to escort him out.

A frown crossed her *tio*'s forehead, and he raised his head and locked eyes with her. "How will we get home? Have you already called a taxi?"

Eva and Jolissa exchanged glances. Eva's encouraging smile and nod enabled Jolissa to explain. "*Tio*," she said, kneeling down beside him, "Eva—my *abuela*—has a car."

Joseph raised his eyes to Eva's before returning them to his niece. "So she will drive us?"

"Actually, *Tio* . . ." Jolissa paused one last time, and then dived in. "I'll be driving. I've been driving *Abuela* in her car for a while now. In fact . . ." She laid her hand on *Tio*'s arm. "*Abuela* has given me the car. It's mine now, *Tio*. We just have to go down to the DMV and take care of the paperwork."

He raised his head again. "You . . . gave your car to my niece?"

"Your niece is now my granddaughter, Joseph," Eva answered. "And yes, I gave it to her. She needs a car to drive, and I don't. It's just that simple."

Tio shook his head and returned his gaze to Jolissa. "Another miracle, *mija*."

Jolissa laughed out loud and kissed his cheek. "Yes, *Tio*. Another miracle for sure."

THEY HAD DROPPED OFF EVA so she could take care of Mario, and then Jolissa and Joseph had headed home. She'd fixed him a light supper of soup and salad, reminding him of his need to eat healthier and pleasantly surprised that he didn't fight her about it; and now she helped him settle into bed for the night.

"Do you need anything else, *Tio*? Am I forgetting anything?" She took inventory of the items within easy reach of his bed: water, a reading light and magazine in case he couldn't sleep, and a newly purchased cell phone, a perfect match to the one she now carried. "You know you can call me anytime if you need me. You just press 2 and hold it down until you hear it ring. I'll come right away. And tomorrow, I'll pick *Abuela* up and bring her here before I go to work. Then I'll leave my cell phone with *Abuela* in case—"

He raised his hand and interrupted her. "I'm fine, *mija*. I have everything I need. Everything. And I understand perfectly what to do with the phone. You just go on to bed and don't worry about me. Get some sleep. I know you're tired and you have to go to work in the morning."

She hesitated. "Are you . . . sure? I mean, there isn't anything else you need or want . . .?"

A light seemed to come on in his dark eyes, and he smiled. "Maybe there is one thing . . . if you still have it and don't mind loaning it to me."

Jolissa couldn't imagine what it might be. "Of course, *Tio*. What is it?"

"I remember your mother left her Bible with you. Do you know where it is?"

Her heart soared. "I do. Absolutely, I do! And I will be happy to get it for you." She started to leave the room to retrieve it, but Joseph stopped her.

"Wait. Please, *mija*."

She turned back to see him pat the side of the bed. "Come and sit here. There is much I must say to you."

Her heart raced, as a slow heat crept up her cheeks. She forced herself back to his bedside and sat down, her emotions tumbling and jumping inside her.

"That Bible is one of the few things I let you keep when you came to live with me."

Jolissa could see the regret on her uncle's face as he spoke. She took his hand and waited.

"Did you never wonder why you didn't end up with more things from your parents?" He shook his head. "No, you were too young to think of such details. Your heart was broken, and you cried yourself to sleep each night." Tears pooled in his own eyes as he spoke. "Yes, I heard you. And I knew I should go in and comfort you. But I just . . . couldn't. I was so . . . scared."

Jolissa started at the thought. Scared? Her *tio*? Why? What in the world did he have to be scared about?

"I know. It makes no sense. But I was. Your mother was my big sister. I was the baby in the family. I'd never been around kids much. And when you came to me, I was still getting used to life in a wheelchair. I couldn't imagine how I'd ever take care of you. I wondered if you would have been better off in foster care and even thought about sending you there, but . . ." He squeezed her hand as a lone tear spilled from his eye and trickled down his cheek. "But you were family. I couldn't do it. You and I . . . we were all that was left of our family. Everyone else was gone. Just you and me. I couldn't send you away, so . . . I kept you."

He hung his head as he went on. "I can't tell you how many times I regretted that . . . not for my sake, but for yours." He lifted his eyes, and an incredible depth of sadness cried out to her. "It was fear, *mija*. Fear that drove me to treat you so badly. I was afraid I wouldn't be able to raise you right, to teach you the things you needed to learn, to keep you out of trouble. I heard so many horror stories of young girls getting into all kinds of problems, and I didn't want that to happen to you. So I pushed you and criticized you and belittled you, hoping to frighten you into staying at home and staying out of trouble." The rest of the tears spilled from his eyes then. "Oh, *mija*, I was so wrong. That was no way to treat such a sweet little girl. I knew I was wrong when you started stuttering almost immediately after you came to live with me, but I just couldn't bring myself to be kind or gentle with you. I am so very sorry, sweet Jolissa. So very sorry. Can you ever forgive me?"

Jolissa was crying by then too, and she leaned toward her *tio* and gathered him into her arms. "Oh, *Tio*, I did already, remember? I already forgave you. How could I do anything else, after God has forgiven us both so freely?"

Between sobs, Joseph whispered, "More miracles. He is a God of many miracles."

She nodded, her head resting on her *tio*'s chest as she listened to his heartbeat and thanked God for giving them more time together.

* * *

JOLISSA STEERED THE CAR BACK TOWARD HER HOME, bringing *Abuela* to spend the day with her *tio*. It was a great relief for her to know that her uncle wouldn't be alone while she was at work.

"The visiting nurse association called very early this morning and said someone would be coming by before noon to help with *Tio*'s care."

"Good, though I'm not concerned. Joseph and I will get along just fine."

Jolissa smiled. She had no doubt that was true.

"*Mija*, I bought your *tio* a present."

Jolissa raised her eyebrows. "Really? How sweet of you, *Abuela*! What is it?"

She heard Eva rustling the paper bag she'd carried into the car with her. "Here it is," she announced.

Jolissa turned her head to see her *abuela* holding up a black leather Bible. "I even had his name put on it: *Joseph Vega*. You can see it when you're not driving. Look back at the road now, *mija*."

Realizing she'd been staring at the Bible, she quickly turned her attention back where it belonged. "*Abuela*, it's beautiful! But when did you have time to get his name put on it?"

The old woman chuckled. "Actually, it was last week, before he ended up in the hospital."

Jolissa nearly slammed on the brakes so she could stop and look Eva in the face. She resisted the temptation and continued driving. "But, *Abuela*, how did you know?"

"I didn't. But God did. Just before that I had asked you for your *tio*'s last name. Remember?"

Thinking back, she did remember now, but it seemed just a curious question at the time. Her *Abuela* never ceased to surprise her.

"And so you went right out and bought a Bible with his name on it."

"As soon as I was certain that's what God was telling me to do, yes. He also told me I would know when the time was right to give it to him. This morning I knew it was time."

Jolissa shook her head in amazement. "Well, you are certainly right about that. Just last night *Tio* asked if he could borrow the little Bible my mom left me. I was thrilled, of course, but I missed not having it to read when I went to bed." She flashed a quick smile in Eva's direction. "Now we will both have one."

Abuela laid a hand on Eva's arm. "Never let anyone tell you God doesn't care about details, because He does—not details centered on our own selfish desires and purposes, but details centered on His purposes, which are never selfish."

Jolissa smiled as she pulled up in front of her home where *Tío* waited. The more she learned about this God who had rescued her, the more she loved Him.

Epilogue

By Saturday, Joseph was feeling stronger and spending more time out of bed. He had even promised Jolissa that he would start using the chair-exercise DVD she'd bought him if she promised not to laugh at him when he did.

She smiled now, as she closed the door to his room, knowing he would sleep for a couple of hours. They'd had a nice lunch together, and she was looking forward to a little alone time to do some studying and also spend some time with her Father.

She was about to settle into her room with her books when she sensed a tug to her old hideaway in the alley. It seemed she hadn't been out there in ages, though it had really been only a few weeks. But the pull was strong, so she picked up her Bible and headed out the back door.

The early afternoon sun was warm overhead, but not nearly as sweltering as it had been the day Jolissa had escaped out here to think of the little girl with the big, sad eyes. The child's face now fresh in her mind, she prayed for Lupita as she crawled inside her former haven and leaned against the fence, her knees pulled up against her chest and her Bible clasped in both hands. Words from drifted into her mind, and she opened to the bookmarked page.

"He who dwells in the secret place of the Most High," she read aloud, "shall abide under the shadow of the Almighty.

I will say of the LORD, 'He is my refuge and my fortress; My God, in Him I will trust.'"

She stopped reading and closed her eyes. "I don't need this old hideaway anymore, do I, Lord? You're my refuge and fortress now, my secret place."

Peace flooded her heart, and she smiled. "All right, then. It's time to get rid of this outdated hideaway once and for all."

She crawled outside, stood to her feet, and set her Bible down on a fence post. An image of a blind Fanny Crosby flashed through her mind, and Jolissa was certain the queen of gospel songs was smiling. Jolissa grabbed the old gate that enclosed her former hiding place and gave it a couple of hard yanks until it came loose from its makeshift moorings. Then she laid it in a pile of other discarded items beside a nearby dumpster.

Picking up her Bible, she began to hum "Blessed Assurance, Jesus Is Mine" as she went back into the house to check on her *tio*.

THE END

OTHER BOOKS IN THIS SERIES

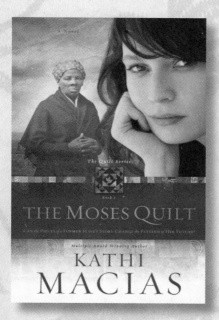

THE DOCTOR'S CHRISTMAS QUILT

(The "Quilt" Series Book #2)

ISBN-13: 9781596693883

N134129

$14.99

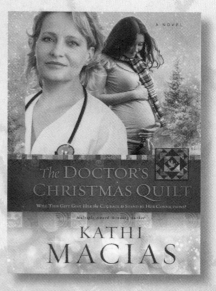

THE MOSES QUILT

(The "Quilt" Series Book #1)

ISBN-13: 9781596693586

N134101

$14.99

FREE downloadable book club guides available
for your book club or small group at NewHopeDigital.com!

Available in bookstores everywhere.

Acknowledgments

We acknowledge the following references and resources in the writing of *The Singing Quilt*:

Fanny J. Crosby, *Fanny J. Crosby: An Autobiography* (Peabody, MA: Hendrickson Publishers, Inc., 2008).

Edith L. Blumhofer, *Her Heart Can See: The Life and Hymns of Fanny J. Crosby* (Grand Rapids, MI: Wm. B. Eerdmans Publishing Co., 2005).

Wikipedia, s.v. "Fanny Crosby."

New Hope® Publishers is a division of WMU®, an
international organization that challenges Christian believers
to understand and be radically involved in God's mission.
For more information about WMU, go to wmu.com.
More information about New Hope books
may be found at NewHopeDigital.com
New Hope books may be purchased at your local bookstore.

Use the QR reader on your
smartphone to visit us online at
NewHopeDigital.com

If you've been blessed by this book,
we would like to hear your story.
The publisher and author welcome your comments and
suggestions at: newhopereader@wmu.org.